THE TUSK
THAT
DID THE
DAMAGE

ALSO BY TANIA JAMES

Atlas of Unknowns
Aerogrammes

The Tusk
That
Did the
Damage

TANIA JAMES

Harvill Secker
LONDON

1 3 5 7 9 10 8 6 4 2

Harvill Secker, an imprint of Vintage,
20 Vauxhall Bridge Road,
London SW1V 2SA

Harvill Secker is part of the Penguin Random House group of companies whose
addresses can be found at global.penguinrandomhouse.com.

Copyright © Tania James 2015

Tania James has asserted her right to be identified as the author of this
Work in accordance with the Copyright, Designs and Patents Act 1988

First published by Harvill Secker in 2015

www.vintage-books.co.uk

A CIP catalogue record for this book is available from the British Library

ISBN 9781846559532

Printed and bound by Clays Ltd, St Ives Plc

Penguin Random House is committed to a sustainable
future for our business, our readers and our planet.
This book is made from Forest Stewardship
Council® certified paper.

FOR RACHEL KURIAN AND MARIAKUTTY LUKOSE,

THE MATRIARCHS

COLONEL HATHI: A Man-cub! *[picking up Mowgli with trunk]* Oh, this is treason! Sabotage! I'll have no Man-cub in my jungle!

MOWGLI: It's not *your* jungle!

—from the 1967 Disney film The Jungle Book

There is nothing left of my home
so I carry my home with me

—Lisa Ciccarello, "One Way of Doing Battle"

THE TUSK
THAT
DID THE
DAMAGE

The Elephant

He would come to be called the Gravedigger. There would be other names: the Master Executioner, the Jackfruit Freak, the great Sooryamangalam Sreeganeshan. In his earliest days, his name was a sound only his kin could make in the hollows of their throats, and somewhere in his head, fathoms deep, he kept it close.

Other memories he kept: running through his mother's legs, toddling in and out of her footprints. The bark of soft saplings, the salt licks, the duckweed, the tang of river water, opening and closing around his feet. He remembered his mother taking him onto her back before launching herself from the bank. In this way, their clan would cross, an isle of hills and lofted trunks.

Among them were two males, a broody old tusker and a twelve-year-old with ivory stubs he was always admiring with the tip of his trunk. As they roamed, the tusker brought up the back of the clan, but if a man were scented somewhere in the vicinity, the cows dropped their doings and circled the two tuskers. They knew what man was after. They offered their rumps instead.

They had walked the same routes for years, this clan, routes that the Forest Department would carve into foot trails of its own. They knew every bend and border, each rutted skull and bull they would meet along the way. But the Gravedigger hadn't learned all there was to learn. His trunk, being stout and clumsy, couldn't sense what his mother's could sense—the sudden stillness in the rhythm of things, the peril in the air.

§

The Gravedigger was a few years old when it happened, still new to the world, but old enough that his mother had gone and calved another one. The newborn was a clumsy little cowpat. She toddled within the pillars of his mother's legs precisely where he used to toddle. Whenever he tried to double back and regain her shade, his mother grumbled and nudged him onward with her trunk. If he fell behind, she flicked her tail until he grasped it, the two walking in tandem, ever in touch.

They emerged from the forest cover to the murky, algal smell of the lake. The water opened wide before them. The Gravedigger was first to splash into the lake, while the cowpat balked at the edge creeping darkly toward her feet. The old tusker slung his trunk into the air and dashed water over his spine.

Toward dusk, they roamed up the mountainside. Shola forest melted into grassland, staked here and there with shrub and tree built stout to withstand the cool. The wind had slackened by then and did not carry down to them, as it usually would, the smell of the man waiting among the branches of an evergreen.

.   .   .

A blast split the silence. The Gravedigger staggered, caught in a carousel of legs and screaming. The man in the tree was pointing a long-snouted gun. Another blast—the tusker bellowed deep and doomed. The Gravedigger whirled in search of his mother, and when at last he caught her scent, he found her roaring in the face of the gunman who aimed into her mouth and shot.

Her head snapped back. Her front feet lifted off the ground for one weightless moment, before lowering, folding beneath her. The whole of her sank with a thud that traveled the earth and ran like a current into the tender slabs of the Gravedigger's soles.

He went to her. He touched her warm trunk, stretched straight but slack. He touched its ridges and folds, and the very tip, a single, empty finger with which she had pinched him a gooseberry not two hours before. A charred scent from her wound. No air from her nostril, no light in the eye.

All around: the stink of gunmetal and smoke.

He watched as two men climbed over the old tusker's face. They pushed and pulled a saw across the bridge of the trunk. Blood spilled over their hands, over the air, as the trunk rolled limply to the ground. They chiseled at one side of a tusk, chipping at flesh, and knocked a hammer on the other side, some chipping, some knocking, until they gently tipped the tusk from the root, easy as a fruit.

.   .   .

They did this to the tusker and the almost-tusker, neatly and quietly opening each face. And then they noticed him.

One man strode toward the Gravedigger, his hair smelling of a sticky odor, some chemical scent mixed with pineapple rot. With the man's every step, the world seemed to tighten. He was holding a knife.

The Gravedigger smelled urine streaming down his leg. He pressed himself against his mother's still warm belly and waited to die.

The man walked past the Gravedigger, around his mother's flank. The Gravedigger could not see what the man was doing. All he heard was the soft squeal of the knife. All he smelled was the pineapple rot.

At last the man rounded her body again and walked away, back to his people. A severed tail flicked from his fist, beckoning.

The Poacher

Everyone in Sitamala thinks they know my brother's story. On the contrary. They may know the tune, but I would bet a half bag of pepper the words are all wrong. I blame his wife's people for spreading slander, all those perfidious huge-hipped sisters, not a one half as lovely as Leela.

Our father was a rice farmer. He came from a time when to farm was a noble profession, when people sought our gandhakasala and our rosematta for their earthy fragrance superior to the stuff that now comes cheap from Vietnam. Who can remember those times with all these farms lying fallow and many a farmer's son gone to roost in a soft office chair? And who am I to blame them, I who have seen the Gravedigger for myself and felt its breath like a steam on my face?

Some say my brother stepped into the very snare he laid for the elephant. I say opinions are cheap from far. I will take you to the Gravedigger myself and let you meet its honey-colored eye. I will show you the day it first laid its foot on our scrawny lives. Then you tell me who was hunter and who was hunted.

§

To know our troubles, you must know what happened to my cousin Raghu. When I think on poor Raghu, I see him stoking a small fire. I see him nudging a stick aside so as to let the flames breathe. I have called up this image many a time as if I were with him in the palli as I should have been that night.

The palli was a paddy-roofed matchbox on bamboo legs stranded in the midst of his father's rice field, same as the ones in the neighboring fields. If a herd of elephants were to come glumping their way through the stalks, we were to wave the lantern and give the long caw that would set the others cawing. If this didn't scare the herd away, we used crackers and rockets. But the herds became wise to our ways. They learned that our racket had no teeth to it, so they kept on eating their way through six months' worth of our back-bent work. Sometimes we had to call the Forest Department; it would send three or four men to blind the beasts with headlights and fire ancient rifles. We called them greenbacks for their dingy green uniforms and their love of currency.

The herds were mostly cows, and they meant no personal harm unless you tampered with a calf. There is no one more fearsome than a mother enraged. In my youth I heard of a cow that cradled the carcass of her baby for days and would not be deprived of it.

Now the solo bull could be a very rude intruder. If one of those fellows were to pay us a visit, we were to leap out of the palli and race home. Do not be fooled by the lumps you see at the zoo—the elephant can run! Ask Raghu's father, who was only twenty years old when a bull elephant discovered him dozing in the palli. Synthetic Achan survived because he knew the elephant has weak eyes. Run straight and you will be trampled. Cut a zigzag and you may confuse it.

Synthetic Achan felt Raghu was too young to sit guard in the palli alone, so he drafted me also. Yet I do not know where I was that night, probably testing my luck with some soft-bottomed girl. What to say. I was nineteen and had discovered that my visage had an effect on certain girls, so to speak. I pretended not to care about my visage, but Raghu needled me about the cream I occasionally raked through my hair. Sometimes he called me Styleking as in: "Eh Styleking, did you bathe in Brylcreem or stick the whole tub up your rump?"

"Yamini likes it."

"Up the rump?"

"Do not talk of her rump."

"I hear what I hear. And from the particulars, I would not touch her with a boatman's pole."

We bickered, but there was a comfort to our fuggy odors and the flash of our teeth in the dark. Other times we burrowed into the quiet, each of us privately wondering what kind of future awaited us. I had a habit of dozing, which Raghu allowed to a limit and would shake me awake only if I were to poof. "What is this," he would shout, flapping his hands about his face, "your personal shithouse?"

Whenever he gently tapped me awake, I knew I had been murmuring for my brother, something like *Where is Jayan where is he,* even though Jayan had been home for six months already. To spare me the shame, Raghu would only say I had been poofing again.

Humble as it was, our palli commanded a five-star view. To the north a phone tower climbed the sky. To the east an owl glared from its bamboo perch, swiveling its head for rodents among the stalks. To the west we watched the sunset pour over the teak-rimmed forest aka Kavanar Wildlife Park.

Our people had been walking the forest long before it took

that fussy name. The new laws forbid us from doing anything in the park, not walking, not even picking up a finger length of firewood without being fined for trespass and stealing. Stealing from trees that had dropped us fruit and firewood for centuries! Meanwhile, the laws looked kindly on the greenbacks and timber companies, their rows of rosewood, eucalyptus, teak.

So I had zero patience for Raghu's ramblings when he decided to tell all about the spectacle he had witnessed one day prior, starring his brand-new hero: Ravi Varma, Veterinary Doctor. I had never seen this Ravi Varma, M.D., though I had heard of his exploits with the greenbacks, and I was no fan of theirs nor his by association.

And what heroic feats had the cow doctor performed to deserve Raghu's worship? Pulled an elephant calf from a tea ditch, where the wee thing had tripped and fallen much to its mother's distress.

I told Raghu my demented old mammachi could pull an elephant calf from a tea ditch.

"Not only that," Raghu enthused. "The vet doctor got the mother to *take back* the baby."

Now this part was pure lie. "A mother elephant won't touch a calf that was handled by humans. Every idiot knows that."

"But she did! And she thanked him after."

"Did they shake hands too?"

"And two sayips were there, filming it all. BBC people I think."

This gave me pause. In those days, it was rare to see foreigners in our parts, and we were neither poor enough nor princely enough to appear on Western screens. I was minimally intrigued. What did the BBC want with us?

Raghu sighed, still dazzled by the memory of Ravi Varma, M.D. "It was something, Manu, I tell you."

Was Raghu musing about the mother and calf on his final evening? Did that sentimental memory lead him to lay down his guard? I imagine his last and lonesome hour, I see him drifting off, a breath from sleep, before he sits up quick to the snap of a broken branch.

In the silence he looks from one doorway to the other. He can open his lungs and caw and set the other pallis cawing, but what if it was only the snap of the fire? He hears me scoffing in his ears: *A broken branch in the middle of a field?*

Raghu hunkers beneath his blanket, hiding from the possibilities.

After a noiseless minute he can breathe again, relieved he never set to squawking like some half-brained bird. He draws deep on the comfort of woodsmoke, sure I will come. Until then, he will tend the fire alone.

The Filmmaker

A long time ago, when the mountains bristled with forest, a boy emerged from the woods and came upon a white man with china-blue eyes. The white man was a British engineer, sent to cut a royal road through the mountains, but he couldn't find a path. He wasn't an explorer, and this was some dense and secretive terrain. Couldn't the boy, being a local and privy to local secrets, just show him the way?

The boy demanded cash and the watch on the engineer's wrist.

Proffering the watch—cash later—the engineer trailed the boy into the mountains, tracing a route tamped by elephant feet. Every so often the boy stopped and said he had to go home because his mother was waiting; he hadn't the time to go all the way to the peak. Just a bit farther, the engineer kept urging, just a bit more.

At sundown they reached the peak. The man squinted at the mountains beyond and smiled as if he'd come into some great inheritance. Happy now? the boy said. Now give me my money.

Just a minute, said the engineer, reaching into his coat pocket.

I don't have any more minutes, the boy insisted.

True, said the engineer, leveling his pistol, and shot the boy in the face.

The engineer slipped the watch off the dead boy's wrist. He thought about the bigger watch he'd buy once the road was built and named after the Englishman who had single-handedly found a route through the ghats.

As it turned out, the bullet gave the dead boy all the time in the world. Many years later, his spirit took up residence in the hollows of a banyan, along the road the engineer had built, and overturned cars as a means of revenge. Only when a priest wrapped the tree in chains was the spirit contained, and cars could once again barrel freely round the bend. Thereafter it was known as the Chain Tree.

§

I leaned out the taxi window to catch a glimpse of the Chain Tree. I'd heard the legend on my first day at Kavanar Wildlife Park and was expecting a hulk more twisted and mythic. In fact, the banyan looked benign, with chains dangling like party streamers from the branches.

The road itself was far more intimidating, all rubble and rollick and switchback. Our taxi driver seemed to think himself invincible, maybe even immortal, the way he dodged cars, scooters, lorries, mini-lorries, tipper-lorries, and a band of pedestrians with hankies tied round their mouths, to fend off dust. A rosary hanging from the rearview mirror spanked the back of the driver's hand. He took no heed of the rosary, or of the road signs that every so often shot by:

BE A CARELESS OVERTAKER
END UP AT THE UNDERTAKER

I was nervous about the shoot; the signs didn't help. Beside me, Teddy sat staring out his window, placid and daydreamy.

"We should've rented a second camera," I said.

"Then who would do sound?" Teddy said.

"Mount a mic on the camera. People do that all the time."

Teddy frowned at the idea. He was a purist about sound quality, though he rarely volunteered to take sound himself.

"I don't know how we're going to get everything with just one camera," I said.

"We're not going to get everything, Em. Once you accept that, it's really liberating."

"Are you going Buddha on me?"

Teddy didn't answer, thus had gone Buddha. Going Buddha was central to his process, rendered him able to cruise into a frenetic situation armed only with a camera and instinct. Neither of us knew what the shoot would entail, but a rescue mission involving elephants was destined for frenzy.

We careened through plantations of coffee and tea, rows of bushes ribboning over the shallow slopes, bedazzled with bright red berries. A silver oak shimmied against the wind, its trunk a smear of marigold fungus. Easier to miss were the ditches carved around the plots, meant to keep wild elephants from snacking on the berries. From time to time, a mother and calf would loot the bushes, and the calf would slip and tumble into a ditch, out of its mother's reach.

This was where Dr. Ravi Varma and his team would intervene. This was what had obsessed me for a year, what Teddy and I had taken three planes and a train to film.

I was the one who'd brought the idea to Teddy in the first place. Fresh out of college, we'd been looking for a subject for our first documentary feature when I learned about Ravi from an in-flight magazine. The photos of fuzzy elephant calves hooked me for the usual cutesy reasons; the description of the veterinary doctor glowed with dramatic potential.

Dr. Ravi Varma spends his days, and most nights, at the Wildlife Rescue and Rehabilitation Center in Kavanar Wildlife Park. His most prized possessions include his camouflage sneakers, his mediocre rum, and his twelve charcoal T-shirts. He prefers charcoal ever since he made the mistake of wearing white to an elephant calf reunion. The mother elephant spotted him easily, bright as a bulb amidst the green, and gave chase.

I learned that Ravi Varma was the head veterinary doctor at the Wildlife Rescue and Rehabilitation Center, known for his roughrider methods at animal rescue. He had pioneered the "calf reunion," a technique that few vets dared to attempt on stranded elephant calves.

"There is a common fallacy here that elephants will reject any baby touched by human hands," Varma said. "What we have learned is the reunion must be instant—speed is the key."

We tracked down Dr. Varma, and after a slew of calls, he reassured us that there would be no shortage of rescues and calamities to film. I sent off a handful of grant applications and won two. Teddy's father, a hand surgeon, bought him a camera and sound kit that outpriced my car. In the fall of 2000, we flew to South India with equipment bags slung over our shoulders, all of which airport security examined slowly and grimly.

For the past few months, Teddy and I had been living at the Rescue Center, a period of Pax Romana in which zero calamities had taken place, resulting in footage that had all the depth and nuance of a promo video. Once or twice—and much to my dread—Teddy had suggested that we include a Morgan Freeman–esque voice-over, a tall order, as Morgan Freemans do not grow on trees. "You have a nice voice, you could do it," said Teddy, but I'd tried voice-over once before and was mortified when the playback revealed the voice of a breathy mouse performing spoken word. No way in hell would I try that here. I wasn't expecting perfection from the film, but I wanted to stand behind every frame, every choice. Other people my age had reels and résumés; all I wanted was a single work that could speak for me, even if that work was a little uneventful.

We were set to leave for the States in two weeks when, in a last-minute break, Ravi called us from his mobile, already on his way to the calf rescue. Here at last was the disaster Teddy had been waiting for, back when a fallen calf was the biggest disaster we could imagine.

By the time we arrived, Ravi's team had been working for three fruitless hours. We edged through the men who had gathered to watch. Teddy raised his camera, but all I could see was a dozen lushly haired crowns, not a bald spot among them, a phenomenon Ravi proudly attributed to coconut oil.

Teddy moved through the crowd with a detached yet pleasant expression, as if accustomed to being two feet taller than everyone around him. I was just as conspicuous with my coppery bun, my yellow Windbreaker, my boom—a long-handled mic with a furry wind guard angled at the end. Whenever we filmed, I expected everyone to turn and surround us like magnet filings to steel, but at present all eyes were fastened on the cow elephant in the distance.

She was hovering over the edge of the ditch. I couldn't see the calf, wedged somewhere inside. The elephant flapped her ears at us, as distressed by her fallen calf as by the shore of our tiny, leery eyes.

I questioned a man whose button-down shirt, a psychedelic weave of pink and orange, suggested a knowledge of English. Puffing up before the lens, the man said a baby elephant was in the ditch, and the Forest Department had already spent a battery of blanks to scare away the mother and rescue the calf. The mother was unbudgeable, kept crying out and tossing clods of dirt into the ditch, as if to build a ramp. "She is very upset, see. And if these Forest Department people get too close, she will abandon the calf. Once the human touches the baby . . ." He shook his head, clasped his hands behind his back. "Mother will leave it behind, no question."

"So then what happens to the calf?"

"It will be captured, trained, and on like that."

We watched the elephant rummage her trunk through the ditch. I'd been looking at elephants so long I forgot sometimes what a magical organ the trunk was, like an arm exploding out from the middle of the face, packed with enough muscle to knock down a tree, enough control in its tiny, tapering finger to grip a lima bean. But even that miraculous limb couldn't save the baby. The mother stood there, withering before our eyes. Huge and forlorn, pugnacious and bewildered.

I managed to say thanks before Teddy hustled me toward the crowd near Ravi's van. He was sitting in the back, hefting onto his lap a caboodle of vials and jars, needles of nightmarish length. Teddy scooched into the van and swung the camera onto the oglers at the bumper, while I extended my mic, adjusted the dials on the DAT at my hip.

"Aha," Ravi said, without looking up. "The media."

Months of almost daily filming had put Ravi at ease with the camera, attuned to the sort of information we needed, the sound bites that would pop on-screen. He lectured, unprompted, while plugging a syringe into a small jar of clear fluid. "This is xylazine-ketamine, for the tranquilizer gun. Tranq is only the backup option. First we try the rubber bullet."

"Why not start with the tranq?" I asked. Teddy homed in on his hands: deftly twisting, injecting.

"She could fall, break a leg. And what if she is still asleep when we get the calf out? We can't babysit the thing; she won't take him back."

The crowds parted for Ravi, their reverential eyes on the tranq gun. He summoned a huddle of forest officers and Bobin, his assistant. (At first, the name "Bobin" had sounded to me like a clerical error, but as Ravi's wiry sidekick, Robin to his Batman, Bobin sort of made sense.)

With Ravi in the lead, the team waded into the aisles between the bush rows, guns raised. The crowd had turned quiet. Teddy had flipped out the camera's LED screen, glancing up and down between screen and ditch.

The elephant swung her body around, squaring herself with us, and at once her fear and fury plunged through me, something buried in the bones, whetted on years of running from men with guns. She growled low, whipping her ears; the men closed in. Only Bobin moved unarmed, some rope contraption coiled around his shoulder, a badge of sweat on his lower back.

At Ravi's shout, a forest officer fired the rubber bullet. Missed.

In answer, the elephant opened her lungs and screamed. My stomach dropped; my dials hit the red zone.

Another gunshot—the elephant's rear leg buckled. The rubber bullet had caught her in the haunch. She fled, hobbling, and the team was sprinting to the ditch and before anyone could tell us otherwise, Teddy and I were sprinting too.

The calf was on its back, stubby legs held aloft. It bleated, dazed, while Ravi and Bobin tugged a sling around its torso and, with the help of the team, dragged the calf aboveground. It lay on its side, panting. The mother bellowed from afar. As Bobin undid the harness, Teddy knelt to the level of its eye, a black magnet to Bobin's every move.

Finally, the team propped the calf on its feet. Ravi barked at the others to flee. He grabbed my arm, the mother thundering toward us. I called for Teddy, still running, unsure if he was behind me or beside the calf, and getting no response I wrenched my arm free, even as the elephant's thud was still hammering from beneath the earth.

I turned to see Teddy filming. The camera was fixed to his chest in order to steady the shot. His face was rigid with fear, barely breathing or blinking as the elephant trundled up to her calf. Twenty yards stretched between Teddy and the elephants, a distance the mother could have closed in seconds. Yet he stood there, as still and spellbound as the rest of us.

The cow touched the calf on the crown, the nape, the wobbly trunk, which lifted, weakly, like a question mark. Her trunk ministered to his in ways at once intimate, familiar, mysterious.

The mother elephant raised her head, leveling her gaze upon Teddy. What happened next would become a subject of debate during an NPR interview, the question of whether the elephant's gesture was, as Teddy would claim, a sign of gratitude. His fellow guest, a quippy animal ethologist, would dismiss the claim, accusing Teddy of "*human*-centric assumptions of animal consciousness."

"That *wave*, as Ted here put it, could have meant anything. It could have been a sign of anger, even warning. It could have been joy. But gratitude is a human expression, learned by hand-reared creatures. I mean, look," the ethologist would add, with so baffled a laugh it was like Teddy had claimed the elephant had curtsied, "a wild animal does not say thanks!"

I would have locked horns with that guy. Had he ever watched a calf suckle its trunk while it slept, whimpering from some secret dream? Had he ever watched Juhi, the oldest girl calf and self-assigned matriarch, drape her trunk over the youngest at a stranger's approach? I'd witnessed these moments on my occasional solo shoots, though none would make it into the final cut. By then it was Teddy's film, the whole thing practically shorn of my presence. I used to believe I was blindsided by how it happened, but I should've seen where I stood, ever at the periphery of things.

The confrontation lasted only a few moments. The mother

elephant whipped her trunk up and down, three deliberate times. Teddy held the shot long after she turned and glided on, her calf in tow, a blot barely higher than the bushes on either side. Through my headphones, I heard the shivering leaves and, beneath that, at a frequency felt only by me, a pulse of envy.

The Elephant

Each night the Gravedigger tossed in his sleep. He woke breathless with visions of ropes and rough hands. Rifles fired through his dreams.

His cries woke the girl calf that lay in the cell next to his. She rumbled low and testy through the dark, then fell quickly back to sleep, forelegs bundled, mouth ajar. He closed his eyes, his mother flitting across his lids, as warm and alive as she'd been not five days before. He stared at the girl calf through the web-strewn slats, the pink wedge of her tongue. He stuffed the tip of his trunk into his mouth.

The anakoodu was built of bamboo and dark mossy wood, with a high tin roof that chattered when it rained. A fence split the space into his and hers, each furnished with a stuffed burlap sack and nothing else, only the ghosts of other calves who had come before them. The air sagged with their smells.

During the day, the Gravedigger ran his trunk around the bars. He patted the ropes that bound them together. He climbed up the bamboo with his front feet, reaching his trunk through the slats. His snout closed like a fist around passing scents. Even after he grew tired of climbing, he kept tracing the knots, crisscross, crisscross. It became a thing he had to do, for buried reasons.

§

The pappans were hotheads, buzzing, restless, rotten smelling. Five were assigned to the anakoodu. The Gravedigger hated all but Old Man.

The days began and ended with Old Man, who was not the oldest and yet seemed a higher authority than the others. They worked quickly and carelessly, but Old Man took his time in his steady assessment of the calves. He chiseled their toenails with a metal file. He oiled each crack and crevice. With firm fingers, he found the knots of hurt and rubbed them until the Gravedigger purred and the girl calf whined for her turn.

He was the only pappan who bent low and let them drape their trunks along his neck. He had no trunk with which to return the gesture and staunchly refused to allow their trunk tips into his mouth. Still it was a comfort, to touch and be touched.

Yet touch could be a cruel teacher. One day, Old Man stood before the Gravedigger in the anakoodu. In his fist was a long stick, capped by a metal talon.

!! said Old Man. !!

The Gravedigger stared. Old Man wore a strange new face, hard and blank as a wall. He reached out and tugged sharply on the

Gravedigger's left ear. The Gravedigger squealed, but Old Man kept pulling until the Gravedigger swerved to the left.

!!! said Old Man. !!!

A sharp tug to the Gravedigger's right ear. He squealed, swerved right.

!!

!!!

!

!!!!

On and on until the Gravedigger could extract a meaning from each ugly note. *Left! Right! Stand Still! Kneel!*—the last learned by the whack of the stick across his flanks. Pain pulled his mind to a taut and terrible line, its only goal: to do whatever would prevent the pain.

Only at bathtime did the Gravedigger resist. He knew the bad hour was approaching by the tourists who thronged outside, chattering, buffooning, baring their teeth, cunning as monkeys. Their noises blurred to a hiss, coiling all around him until he could not breathe.

It began with a scraping sound; Old Man slid out two of the wooden boards, the square of sunlight parted by his shape. In the early days, Old Man tied a rope around the Gravedigger's middle in order to tug him to the water. Once the Gravedigger learned not to tug back, to beetle along in silence, the rope was undone.

They proceeded in line: Old Man, the girl calf, the Gravedigger, and two more pappans. There was the spitter, who continually shot red tongues of paan out his mouth, and the squat one, whose breath simmered with liquor. Every so often, either the spit or the squat would bark at the Gravedigger, for reasons beyond his knowing. Sometimes he cut a hot fart to shut them up.

The crowd followed at a distance, clucking along, as all five stumped single file across the open and down a slope. There the trail spread into the riverbank. As soon as the Gravedigger caught a murky, algal whiff, he panicked and tried to turn back, but the pappans shoved him onward.

When they reached the banks, the girl calf trotted into the lake and stopped a few feet shy of Old Man, who took a wide stance on the rocks. Murmuring gently, he tossed water on her back. Occasionally he scooped a handful into his own mouth and gazed out over the breeze-pleated currents. The girl calf glittered in the sun, her hair bejeweled with droplets, her eyes drowsy with pleasure.

The Gravedigger was miserable. They kneed him into the water and tugged on his ear. Again and again they doused him with water, and again he was at the lake with his clan, and there was the tusker tossing water and there was his mother spraying him in the mouth. He burrowed his face into the girl calf's side, but there was no escaping what all he remembered.

§

Twice a day, the adult elephants nodded past the anakoodu on their way to the lake, clanking chains. The pappans rode on their backs or walked alongside.

The first time the Gravedigger had glimpsed all the giants together, he thrust his trunk through the bamboo bars and keened. Cows and cousins of varying browns and grays. He thought he scented his mother among them.

He cried out as they passed, but not a one turned her head, as if they were less than strangers, not even the same kind. Yellow-green urine stained their hind legs. An alarming absence in their eyes.

Every night, the Gravedigger escaped. He closed his eyes and saw himself swimming steadily across the river, led by the scent-seeking periscope of his trunk. He saw himself break the surface and climb onto the opposite bank where his mother was waiting. There he was, his trunk wrapped in hers. Whatever hurt or sorrow befell him was not really happening to him. He was on the other bank with his mother. He was not here.

§

So began the Gravedigger's second life, a tale that would remain incomplete without a proper portrait of Old Man. In the end, the newspaper stories would ignore almost entirely the late T. S.

Mahadevan; some would neglect to mention his name. Yet he would live for another decade in rumors and rhymes, summoned like a spirit that would never know rest.

At the Sanctuary, most of Old Man's days were the same. As overseer, he sat on a bench outside the shack he shared with three others and watched the calves. Two at a time, the calves passed through his anakoodu, where he coaxed and bullied them from the brink of despair. His was an arsenal of soft words and soft blows, plus the odd nugget of sugar. Soon as he roused a calf from near dead, it was yanked from his anakoodu, another pair of needy eyes in its place.

In his lap lay the logbook. His tiny script crawled over every corner, defying the faint blue lines. He turned the crackling pages and scanned the names of his former orphans. Each flickered brief as a firefly in his memory: *Asha, Arjuna, Balram, Balachandran, Ramachandran, Kamini, Ashwini, Saraswati, Omprakash, Ramprakash, Babu Prakash.* So many names and nowhere among them his own.

His father had been pappan to only one elephant, Kannan, for the whole of his life. What Kannan taught Appachen he passed to his son on slow, humid nights such as these. *If an elephant tosses dirt on his back, he is comfortable. If an elephant stands utterly still, he is troubled. An elephant will only lie down to sleep if he trusts the company he keeps.*

T. S. Mahadevan was sixteen years old when he and his father first walked Kannan through the gates of the Sanctuary, after the elephant had been cast off by the temple that had housed him for twenty years. To Appachen, the Sanctuary was hardly an improvement, with its camera-crazy tourists and elephant-shaped trash cans and so-called pappans. Few had learned the trade from their fathers. Most hopped from one job to the next as easily as hopping a bus. All they saw in a grown elephant was its awful strength, enough to split a man in half were he too slow to strike the first blow.

Appachen had long stopped using the pronged ankush on Kannan. They spoke their own private language: a mere word and Kannan would knee him onto his back. One afternoon, they were walking along a highway when Appachen was dizzied by heat and fainted. He later awoke to the living hull of Kannan's chest, contracting and expanding. Kannan had been standing over him to guard against passing cars, a view Appachen would remember forever, as he lay enchanted by the rhythm of that huge, flexing heart.

Stories like these led the pappans to believe that Appachen had something divine about him, some extraordinary talent derived by dark art. Some said he had once stumbled across the fabled elephant graveyard, the field of tusks and skulls no man had seen, and there obtained the gift of elephant insight. Some said he had been an elephant in some long-ago life. Young Mahadevan knew his father to be a vivid storyteller and the likely source of these theories.

But there was no contesting the depth of Appachen's knowledge, which he put to good use in the anakoodu. In those days, half the babies lived briefly, casualties assigned to grief.

. . .

It was Appachen's concoction of baby formula, thickened with ragi and jaggery, that roused most of the calves from near dead, though nothing could be done for the babies that had already begun to recede, limply eating and drinking while the light leaked from their eyes.

The newest calf had come to the Sanctuary with that same draining gaze. The Forest Department had found it on a mountainside, starving beside the dead bulk of its mother. Only her tail had been cut, to be sold as a talisman.

For two weeks, day and night, Old Man watched the calf. It ate little. It was always grasping for Old Man's arm. If Old Man were to step away and trade talk with the field director, the calf would climb up the bamboo slats and cry until Old Man clucked softly, What is it, child?

These days, the calf made not a sound, as if its previous plaintive self were buried somewhere inside this silent creature. How could one so small have the stillness of an older elephant? And why did it cower from the smell of pineapple?

Appachen could not be consulted, having died ten years before, a few months after Kannan. *Cardiac arrest,* the doctor had called it, but Old Man knew the truth. Appachen had spent most of his life as Kannan's pappan, so many years it was no longer clear who was leading whom.

The Filmmaker

Ravi handled the reporters like a pro. Hands in pockets, he fended off praise with an enigmatic smile, ducking further questions. The bystanders practically cheered as he cut to the van, where he ceded shotgun to Bobin in an act of magnanimity.

Here the pleasantries ended.

"What were you thinking?" Ravi said, turning on Teddy. "You make your shot and get out. You don't wait around and get the elephant's autograph."

Teddy offered a blithe apology, still riding high from the shoot. "It was worth it, though, you'll see."

"And if she had crushed you, still it would be worth it?"

"You know she wasn't going to crush me. She wouldn't leave her calf a second time."

"I know elephants. It's you people I don't know, and yet you are my responsibility. So next time I say run, you *run*."

Teddy looked to me for backup. I took some satisfaction in saying, "Ravi's right," to which Teddy gave a petulant snort—*you always take his side.*

I was used to playing referee. Teddy and Ravi were prone to bickering, ever since their first and only interview session. The conversation quickly had turned combative, so much so it had pained me to type the transcript:

TEDDY: We've been discussing human-elephant conflict, but I'm wondering about the bigger picture. What about, for example,

the industrial projects—the mines, the plantations—aren't
these mostly responsible for displacing elephant populations?

RAVI VARMA: Of course.

TEDDY: And many of these projects are permitted by the Forest
Department, with whom you work closely.

RAVI VARMA: Yes.

TEDDY: That seems like a contradiction.

RAVI VARMA: Life abounds with contradiction.

TEDDY: It doesn't bother you?

RAVI VARMA: Many things bother me. Like sayips who come to
India and ask questions to which they have already decided an
answer. That is not an interview. That is a cross-examination.

In this instance, Ravi extended a partial olive branch: "The mate-
rial was good, then?"

"Are you kidding?" Teddy leaned in. I got a noseful of coconut
oil; was Teddy worried about hair loss? "I was so close, I could
hear her breathing."

As the play-by-play went on, I closed my eyes, no match for
the hunger headache drilling my forehead from within. My
mouth was a sand trap, my tongue coated in the orange slime of
my last Tic Tac.

Ravi and Teddy, meanwhile, had forgotten their beef and
were now discussing the reporters and cameras and bystanders,
the public side of Ravi's work. "More than my words," he said,
"they are looking to see how I speak, how I hold myself. People
do not have such a high opinion of vet doctors. They think we
treat cows and buffalos only. My own brothers used to call me
cow doctor—" Glancing at me, he stopped and said with typical
Varmese bluntness, "I think you are bored."

"No, just a little weak. I haven't eaten yet."

"Then we will stop and take some snacks."

Over Teddy's protests, we pulled up to a precariously slanted stall. Ravi got out and returned in moments with a paper bag blotchy with grease.

"These unni appams are famous," he said, pointing the open bag at me. A sweet scent wafted up from the unni appams, heaped like a clutch of warm eggs. Ravi popped one whole in his mouth.

Teddy demurred, retracting into his vest like a turtle. An elephant he could handle, but Teddy lived in fear of food poisoning, always asking for bottled water over boiled, squirting his palms with an antibacterial gel that reeked of first-world caution.

"Not a good idea," Teddy advised me. "Your IBS?"

"IBS?" Ravi frowned, through chews.

Before Teddy could elaborate on my bowels, I reached into the paper bag.

"I'm not trying to be pushy," Teddy said.

"I know. It just comes naturally."

Out of the corner of my eye, I caught Ravi's smirk.

So did Teddy. "Have it your way," he said and got out of the car, taking the camera with him. Bobin strode in another direction, without explanation, which meant he was off to take a semipublic leak.

The unni appam was a spongy parcel of warmth, grease, and banana-flavored sweetness, the color of maple syrup. Ravi looked especially pleased when I reached into the bag for another and matched his grease-lacquered grin.

I waited for Ravi to slip me some weirdly intimate aside. It happened from time to time, when Teddy was out of earshot. *You look like the girl from Dr. Zhivago . . . I like that funny tooth you have . . . Do you have freckles all over?* Once he asked me: "Why do you always wear that windbag?"

"My Windbreaker?" I said. "It has lots of pockets."

"It hides everything."

"That's kind of the point." I could feel myself blush. "I'd rather not draw attention to myself out here."

"Too late for that."

At the time, the banter seemed harmless, maybe even necessary to our dynamic. I conducted all our interviews, drew stories from him that he rarely shared. "You have a way of talking," he told me once, "that makes me forget the camera is there." I thought I could preserve the intimacy he felt around me, keep him loose and trusting, but just when I'd fool myself into thinking I had the upper hand, he'd turn on me with that cutting cobra gaze, and my resolve would go woozy. I'd have to remind myself that we had three weeks left at the Rescue Center; there was no time for crushes, no room for any emotion other than pinpoint focus on the task at hand.

A focus that was hard to maintain when he was leaning against the van, scrutinizing me. I expected him to volley a comment about "American girls" or my funny tooth.

"You and him," Ravi said, glancing at Teddy. "You are the same age?"

"Yeah, why?"

"He treats you like a child. And you let him."

I flinched. "Childlike" was not how I would've described myself. At twenty, I'd driven from Albuquerque to Asheville with only my dad's German shepherd by my side. I resisted lengthy

melodramatic relationships. My longest had lasted four months;
I squashed it after Gus said that a woman driving alone, cross-
country, was basically asking for it. The memory made me bristle
all over again.

"What is he doing?" Ravi asked.

"Filming," I said sharply. In the distance, Teddy was aiming
his camera at a sign that said LIFE HAS NO SPARE. "He's just pro-
tective. You don't know him."

"I know you. I know you have your own mind." Ravi balled
up the paper bag as Bobin approached. "Does he?"

Ravi opened the passenger door, allowing me to climb inside.
The whole way home, I kept stealing glances in the rearview.
I'd spent dozens of hours interviewing him, uprooting his past,
editing his answers, studying every blink and pause and grimace.
And yet there remained a version of Ravi I hadn't seen until now,
the guy who had all along been studying me.

Teddy and I had never been romantic, aside from one recent and
regrettable fling. Ours was a loyalty born of classes and collabora-
tion and NoDoz and nerves, and his brush with expulsion.

We had met in Intro to Film. On our first assignment, we
were sent out into the wilds of Boston with only a tripod, a light
meter, and a hand-crank Bolex camera. Each of us was to shoot
a light journal, to capture light and shadow on black-and-white
sixteen-millimeter film. It was exhilarating—the feel of the Bolex
rumbling between my hands, its spring-wound arm tracing circles in the air.

I came to class burning with anticipation, sure that I'd net-
ted a string of beautiful shots from the reflecting pool at the

Christian Science Plaza. But as we screened our dailies, it was Teddy who stole the show with his time-lapsed shots of shadows fading, darkening, interlacing, pouring like ink across stone, a calligraphic symphony of lines until the film fluttered to white, leaving the whole class enchanted. All this he'd filmed in the courtyard of his dorm.

As the years went by, Teddy and I fell into step, collaborating on every film down to his junior project, for which I served as DP. It began with an exterior shoot on a day so snowy and cold the Aaton camera had to be hugged in blankets every few takes, to keep it from stuttering to a stop. A week later, we screened the dailies to find a thick river of white coursing down the left side of the film. A whole day ruined. I'd been the one to seal and unseal the camera mag, to off-load the film into its can, a process that required nimble hands inside a lightproof bag. Apparently mine hadn't been nimble enough. I was mortified, excuseless, solely responsible.

"So," Teddy had said, rewinding the film, "reshoot on Thursday?"

I couldn't believe he would trust me to shoot again. I'd expected him to demote me to gaffer's assistant, angling a bounce board by the actors' faces.

Teddy shrugged it off. "So you shit the bed. Nothing to freak out about."

Both literally and figuratively, that seemed the perfect reason to freak out.

But with a calm that somehow fed off my frenzy, Teddy insisted that we'd fix it. And what he said next is embedded in my memory, proof that we were once good to each other.

"I'd rather get it wrong with you than get it right with anyone else."

We rolled up to the rusty green gates of the Rescue Center, greeted by a sign: THANKS FOR NOT INSISTING TO SEE THE ANIMALS. An odd marker when there seemed no animals to see, only a storybook hamlet of dark green huts nestled within the leaves, connected by a shaded walkway where one could pause and study the posters of animals on the walls.

The sky was overcast, diffusing a clean cold light through a woolly skein of cloud. I wanted to take advantage of the light and shoot Ravi on his rounds with the animals—the elephant calves, the goat, the langurs who streaked through the air on long, windmilling limbs. But Teddy argued that we'd shot it all before, and what was another langur sequence compared with the final shot he had gotten from the calf reunion? "I think we can even leave it as is," he said. "One long shot, like in that Obenhaus film about the jewelry factory."

He was always referring to That Obenhaus Film About the Jewelry Factory. I'd never seen it but felt like I had, what with all the times he had described the opening—a man punching a time clock, a shot that Obenhaus held for a full minute until the clock hands met, which Teddy called brilliant in its illustration of work and its weight on the passage of time.

"Keep in mind," I said, "we want actual human beings to see this thing."

Teddy followed me into my room. He lived next door to me at the Rescue Center, each "guest suite" appointed with a chair, a desk, and a twin bed on which Teddy could only fit himself diagonally. He set the camera on my desk. "Just watch the dailies tonight."

"Why—where'll you be?"

He unscrewed the filter between careful fingers. "Sanjay's wedding, I told you. You can still be my date."

"Pass."

"Come on, he's not that bad."

Sanjay was Teddy's former roommate, a soft-spoken guy who had renounced alcohol for religious reasons and embraced weed with equal fervor. In stoner mode, he was always making the sort of prickly asides (*Why don't you guys make out already? . . . Get a room!*) that put his own loneliness on display.

I set a pot of water on my hot plate. "I'd rather stick around here," I said. "In case something happens."

"In case what happens?" He slipped the filter into its pouch, nestled the lens inside the camera bag. "We don't need more elephant baths and feedings. It's the human stories that'll read on film."

"Well, and I also need a break from humans."

Teddy looked at me. "Which ones?"

I took my time breaking a cake of ramen, neatly, delicately, into the water.

Two weeks before, Teddy and I had been editing side by side, late into the night, when he leaned over and kissed me. I'd been saying something about the aspect ratio when the kiss cut me off midword, and I remember thinking, as it was happening, that contrary to every rom-com movie I'd ever seen, spontaneity was a poisoned dart to romance; in reality, the kissee needed warning, a questioning look or a leaning in. How weird to be friends for five years and then, in the space of a second, conjoined at the face.

But then the weirdness gave way to an inviting familiarity. He smelled like summer, like sunblock, scents from home. It was comforting more than thrilling, which was what caused me to pull away. Teddy seemed hurt when I asked him to go, but the next day, he returned with a sheepish apology. He understood that this was the wrong place to start something between us, that it was important to maintain an air of professionalism at the Rescue Center. "But we should, you know, revisit this," he said, looking only at his hands. "When we get back home."

I told him there was no need for apology, it was no big deal, hoping all the *no*'s would add up to a subliminal *never*. Whatever comfort I'd felt in that moment of indiscretion had shriveled to a sickening knot; I'd led him down the garden path, as my mother would've put it.

Now, as I forked the wormy noodles apart, I could feel Teddy looking at me with dread, as if he sensed I was about to burn the garden to the ground.

But I couldn't do it. Not then and there. Not when he was my only friend.

Instead I said I wanted to stay behind and log tapes. "See if there's an Oppenheimer in there."

"Obenhaus," he said, reluctantly releasing me from his gaze.

After Teddy left, I planted myself behind my laptop, plugged in the camera, and watched the rescue. The calf was on the ground, waiting to be released from the harness. Teddy zoomed in on the needy eye, the pupil like a fly trapped in sap. That close, I found the eye haunting for reasons unclear: Because I saw something familiar inside, a consciousness I could recognize? Or because I couldn't?

For my fifteenth birthday, my father had bought me a parakeet. I loved Daisy, how her feathers gave off a powdery smell, how her feet embraced my finger with a lightness I took for trust, the shiny droplet of her eye. Sometimes I worried that Daisy was depressed, to which my father suggested I put Prozac in her feed, a joke that annoyed me. Why couldn't Daisy be depressed? Why couldn't she feel a host of emotions, some of them beyond our explanation? She could fly, so if her body were capable of acts beyond human limitation, couldn't her mind be capable of emotions beyond our own, like Wing Boredom or Flock Joy or Plummet Buzz, things we couldn't feel and, therefore, could never understand?

"Maybe you're the one who needs medication," my father said.

During preproduction, I had envisioned a film that would encompass my youthful questions, that would exhume the traumas sealed deep inside animal minds. Day by day, the film I'd imagined seemed to inch a bit farther from the footage we had, until now.

Teddy had been right. The shot would hold its weight on-screen, all sixty-two pulsing seconds, the heart of our film. During the moment of mother-calf reunion, Teddy hadn't fiddled with the zoom, had let the action unfold, giving wide berth to those twining trunks, whose ministrations seemed to suggest comfort and tenderness and yet seemed somehow private, primal, on a plane of communication we could glimpse only indirectly.

I started logging the tape, marking time codes, jotting impressions. The camera followed Ravi through the crowds, into the van, pulled in on his hands. There was something I hadn't noticed at the shoot, amid the commotion and confusion—how calm he was throughout. The showdown could've been set to Morricone, with Ravi as Eastwood moving through the green, arms around the gun. Wolfish, deliberate. I felt myself ambushed by awe.

So when Ravi knocked on my door, around nine, I was slightly starstruck. There he stood, the hero at rest.

"You missed dinner," he said.

"Teddy went to a wedding. I just thought I'd get a head start on today's stuff."

"He left?" Ravi asked, almost hopefully.

"Yeah, he gets back day after tomorrow."

"Then let me take you to dinner."

"Oh." The offer seemed fraught. "Well, I already had noodle soup . . ."

Ravi peered over my shoulder.

"Is that Dev?" On my laptop, an elephant calf filled the screen. Dev was easy to spot with his signature mini-mohawk. "You have more footage of him? Can I see?"

It seemed an innocent request at the time, though, I can admit to myself now, I didn't want it to be.

I stepped aside, and easy as that, Ravi walked into my life.

Ravi had rescued Dev from a cave where a female elephant had gotten herself stuck between boulders. By the time the team found her, she was starving to death, Dev tiny against her ankle, sore spattered and weak. Ravi shouldered Dev like a sack of rice and carried him out. At the center, Dev was too weak to stand, so they propped him over belly slings.

Ravi explained all this from the foot of my bed. We had just watched a sequence of Dev nudging a soccer ball with the other calves, the keepers weaving among them, egging them on.

"What happened to Dev's mother?" I asked.

"We had to leave her. Eventually she starved to death."

"Jesus."

He surveyed my room, his gaze remote, illegible. Maybe he was dismissing my foreign brand of sentimentality; maybe he was a little grossed out by the ganglia of ramen still in the pot. Landing on a thought, he lit up. "Dev will leave for Manaloor in two weeks, to be reintegrated into the park. It's six hours away, but you should go. You should film it."

I envisioned the perfect final shot: three little calves sauntering like cowboys into the sunset. "So we'd spend our last week in Manaloor?"

"Oh, you're leaving." He paused, barely hiding his disappointment. "Already."

"Why don't you come along? To Manaloor, I mean."

"You don't want me there."

"Sure I do."

"No, no, it's the villagers. They would run me out, even though I have nothing to do with that mess . . ." He raked a hand through his hair, deciding whether to tell me or not. I didn't press. I didn't have to. He just started talking.

The villagers were upset—enraged, really—that the Forest Department had subsidized Shankar Timber Company to fell the trees on their forestland. Technically, it wasn't the villagers' land;

all forestlands belonged to the Forest Department (as inherited from the British raj, who had previously claimed all forestlands for the queen). But the villagers of Manaloor felt they deserved some say over the lands where they'd been harvesting firewood and honey long before Queen Victoria was in diapers.

"Mostly they blame Samina Hakim. She is the Divisional Range Officer, the face of the Forest Department." He shrugged. "Ah well. It will pass."

I wanted to know more, but Ravi stood up. I felt a pang of dismay, thinking he was on his way out.

"If you won't have dinner," he said, "at least we can have a drink."

Over coffee spiked with the dubious rum he kept locked in his desk, we talked. The liquor rushed my stomach and turned me loose; I was intoxicated by his presence, enamored with every detail of his life and eager to spill all of mine. I told him of my parents, who watched my films with anxious expressions, as if my work were one long oral exam to which they had no answer. He told me of his parents, who thought he was some kind of Indian Johnny Appleseed, planting trees for a living. Somewhere in that miasma of oversharing was the one story I still wish I hadn't spilled, a name that Teddy would've hated me for spilling.

Shelly Blake.

As a senior, Teddy had made his thesis film about a sophomore named Shelly Blake. She was secretly, feverishly, in love with him, and thus willing to allow him access to anything, including her anorexia. She let him film her weigh-ins, her caffeine supplements, her homemade collage of runway models, her endless jogs. He gave her a camera with which to record "video diaries" on her own time; in one of these, she singed her arm with a lit cigarette.

Shelly attended the end-of-year screening, along with hundreds of students, teachers, people she didn't know. There was more nervous laughter than she had probably anticipated. Afterward she congratulated Teddy, went home, and slit her wrists.

Ravi's eyes widened. "Suicide?"

"Attempted. Her parents filed a lawsuit . . ." I remembered how Teddy had nearly dropped out of school. I remembered him sitting on the edge of his bed, head in his hands, and all at once I realized I'd just betrayed him. "It was a long time ago."

We were silent for a time. My lips felt numb.

"Lot of secrets," Ravi said.

"I won't tell if you won't."

"No?" He gave me a sly look. "You are not recording this?"

"Recording?"

"No hidden cameras, no mics?"

"Not that I know of."

"Good," he said lightly, taking the mug from my hands and setting it on the floor.

My feet were between his feet. I had my mother's pinkie toe, a tiny embarrassing tuber with barely a nail to speak of. A certain energy seemed to rise around my toe and me, my heart gathering speed. He lifted my chin. He kissed me.

I felt my head go light as we stood, as his two cool hands snuck up my shirt, lingering at my waist. I was too fleshy, too pale, unprepared on many levels (grooming included), and yet propelled by desire. There was something about the way he took his time, the way he handled the hook and eye of my bra with one hand. He was as calm and intent as he'd been earlier that day, as if he knew what to do, how it would happen, that all our banter would lead, eventually, to this narrow bed.

"Wait—" I said and sat up, shocked by a hard, vehement pounding, someone's door shaking on its hinges. "What is that?"

"The new calf," Ravi said. "Had to be quarantined."

For such a cute calf by day, the newbie had morphed by night into a battering ram. We listened for a moment to the clanking padlock. My heartbeat returned. I caught Ravi casually assessing my legs and felt a pulse of anticipation. "Ignore it," he said, and soon enough the pounding folded into the white noise, all of it draining away.

Later, he fell asleep with his arm around my waist. I lay wide awake, my back against his chest. The chest of my subject. (Which turned out to be not as hairy as his head hair implied, but sparse and pleasantly scratchy.) By then the liquor had burned off, and what had felt sweetly reckless only hours before had solidified into something irrevocable and real.

I imagined this scene through Teddy's eyes, an exercise that made my stomach buckle. It would seem as though I'd timed my sin precisely around his absence, a calculated plan, not a plunge.

I thought of Teddy, apologizing. *I crossed a line. It's my fault.*

And here I'd not only crossed a line, I'd scaled a great wall. Sleeping with the subject of your film was completely out of bounds, unpardonable, certainly missing from the index of *The Art of Documentary.* Would Ravi expect this to happen again? If I said no, would he close himself off, spurned and wounded? And what if I wanted to say yes?

My thoughts pinballed between all possible scenarios, settling on the greatest likelihood: in a few weeks, we would all part ways. No harm done.

Until then, Teddy could not find out.

I dreaded the next morning, having to clump through an awkward discussion while searching for our underwear. Against what actually happened, such a scenario now seems quaint.

Morning broke like a frying pan in the face, or stomach, rather, where the unni appams had already begun their long and ruthless assault. I traveled between toilet and bed at least three times before Ravi insisted on driving me to a medical clinic. I lay across the backseat of the jeep, my stomach spasming with every thought of those two greasy gobs.

He helped me into the waiting room where a handful of women sat with deadened expressions. One had a child in her lap, a girl with a shaved head and huge kohl-caked eyes. I took a seat across from the mother, who was whipping the end of her sari in breezy circles, and put my two-ton head in my hands.

I met a doctor in a closet-sized examining room. He asked me how I felt; I laid my head like an offering on his desk, an inch from his big, tufted knuckles. I heard him say to Ravi, with vague accusation: "She is dehydrated. Look how pale she is."

Ravi escorted me everywhere, even when I tried to ward him off. He followed me into the doctor's office, to the exam room, and once, regretfully, to the outhouse, from which I emerged horrified by what I'd left behind for some hapless sweeper—*Why wasn't the goddamn faucet working?*—and there was Ravi, like a man dreading a verdict. The world rocked beneath me as I staggered around, half fainted, crawled onto someone's gurney. I registered certain things. The lemur baby from the waiting room, in the lap of her mother. A small square tray of syringes. A burnt smell. The veins in my arms had thinned to pinstripes. A nurse tried feeding an IV into the back of my hand. The first two times, I gritted my teeth against the pain. No luck. The third time, the nurse lanced my flesh and, while inside, went fishing. I screamed FUCKSHITFUCK and dissolved into mortifying tears. In solidarity or dread, the lemur baby began to squall, and my throat thickened up from a certain kind of panic that had nothing to do with fainting and vomit and needles but rather the sense that I had allowed myself to arrive here, alone and sick, a foreigner in a foreign room.

"Breathe," said a voice, a simple order that split the fog.

Ravi stepped forward. He cupped my head with a hand practiced in the art of calming the frantic and the feral. It occurred to me then that he had the jawline of a film star, or at least a prime-time anchorman. It also occurred to me that my panic was optional and that I could expel it, at least partly, with one shaky exhalation.

I watched the IV fill my limb with fluid. The baby grew calm, and her stained face made me want to wipe my own, but Ravi was holding my good hand, and the other lay limp as a glove on my chest.

Guilt made a martyr of Ravi. After we returned from the clinic, he brought me coconuts stuck with flimsy straws. On most Saturday evenings, he had dinner with his mother, but this time he told her there was an elephant calf that needed round-the-clock monitoring. Somehow he got her to make him dinner anyway, a soup of rice with green mango chutney. This he delivered to my bedside, waiterlike, a cotton towel over his arm.

Sunday morning, while Ravi snuffled into my hair, I texted Teddy: *Got sick yesterday. Had to go to hospital. Don't worry.*

Moments later, my cell phone jittered on my desk. Teddy. Ravi stirred, tightened his arm around my waist.

"Are you okay?" Teddy said. "What hospital? Why didn't you call?"

"I'm totally fine," I croaked.

"Was it the dal? Or no—those grease balls!"

Just then, Ravi's cell phone burst into song: the theme from James Bond. He made a lowing noise and rolled out of bed. I flapped a hand at him, pointed at my phone, mouthed *Teddy*.

"Is someone there?" Teddy asked.

Bleary, Ravi trudged to the bathroom and closed the door, answering the call with his usual, "Hah, tell me."

"Uh no, I'm watching a movie." I grasped at vaguely familiar names: *Goldeneye, Goldfinger* . . .

Thankfully, Teddy didn't care for specifics. He said he'd be back by evening, or possibly earlier if he could catch the bus. After we hung up, I wiggled down into the warmth of my covers, listening to the murmur of Ravi's voice. I'd never seen him stay on the phone this long.

At last Ravi emerged and shut the door, slowly, behind him.

"Teddy's coming back," I said with a twinge of disappointment. I brushed a black comma-shaped curl from my pillow. "You're off the hook."

Ravi leaned against the door. "An elephant killed someone," he said. "In Sitamala. Near to my mother's place."

"What? That's terrible."

He nodded, absorbed in thought. There was the distant, drifting silence again, the indecipherable knit of his brow.

"Did you know the person?"

He was speechless so long I thought he hadn't heard me. "I know the elephant," he said finally. "Everyone does."

The Poacher

By morning, the palli was strewn about as if exploded. Roof smashed, legs snapped. At the calm center of this chaos: a pile of thatch laid with care across the body of my cousin.

Raghu's mouth was a hollow of astonishment. From the chest up and hip down he looked unharmed. The middle of him looked like something the elephant had tried to erase.

There were five or six greenbacks on the scene, doing nothing of note. One of them knelt by the elephant's footprint. I expected him to come up with some advanced tracking device, but he pulled a length of string from his pocket and gently laid it round the border of the footprint as if to take the murderer's shoe size.

Those who came to watch pushed in with all manner of theories.

"This is the Gravedigger's work. Who here would forget it? Buries its victims just like this."

"But it hasn't come round in ten years!"

"It feasts on human flesh."

"Are you stupid? Elephants eat greens."

"I hear it eats jackfruit by the bushel, so much you can smell it coming. Death never smelled so sweet."

Raghu's mother was removed from the premises for fear she would scream herself insane asking the same question over and again: What kind of father would send a child of seventeen, *seventeen,* to sit in the palli alone?

"Not alone," he said quietly. His sunken eyes found mine.

My mouth felt dry, my tongue a lump of clay. I saw he blamed me for deserting his only son and the pain of it went through and through me.

Later we cast my cousin's ashes in the Stream of Sins behind the temple. The mountains sat gaunt and blue on the opposite side, watching, as they had done for all time, us grievers and bathers and sinners.

I had thought the ashes would sink with grace. Yet Raghu sat in a stubborn clump on the surface as if to say, *You guilty wretch, you will not be rid of me so easy.*

A wailing went up from the women, though my aunt did not cry; her grief had turned hard and silent. I watched from the banks where Raghu and I had once set sail a boat of string and sticks while our mothers prayed in the temple. There went my friend, my boyhood entire.

I loved my brother equally, but we were not equals, as he was elder to me by five years. Little creature, my mother used to call him, for the pelt of hair he had worn from birth. And there was something creaturely too about the man he became, all sinew and scruff, the way he looked through you like a cool-eyed cat. Being a hunter, Jayan knew things—how to tell between the slots of a sambar and the pug of a tiger, between cow pie and buffalo turd and elephant scat. He had a botanist's knowledge of wild plants, though he had not studied botany or anything else since age fourteen. To him, the forest was the only school worth attending.

Jayan might have made a so-so student had my father shown any interest in discipline. What to say. I suppose my father was too busy making his own mistakes.

By day my father was a farmer; by night, an accomplished drunk, well known to finish a whole bottle of rum and still find his way to another. The drunken part of him we could have managed, shouldering him home on night after stuporous night, thinning the yogurt concoction that would have him back and bloodshot on his feet next morning. Yet he also suffered an unholy weakness for betting on cards, dogs, local elections, anywhere he might turn a note into two. You would not think him weak by his broad back and his woolly beard and his godlike gaze turned inward as if trying to make sense of the world. But it was a weakness of will that made him empty his pockets each night and sell off two of our acres to finance his madness. Weakness that made him swipe my mother's wedding gold, a necklace so long she had looped it thrice around her throat.

"Maybe he needs the money for an investment," I said.

"Maybe someone wants him dead," said Jayan.

"You don't know anything."

"I know he is no saint." From his pocket Jayan pulled a strange piece of metal shaped as four connected loops. He slipped the loops through his fingers and faked a punch at my nose, grinning at my flinch. "This I found in his cabinet." Jayan gazed at his fingers as if admiring a fine piece of jewelry. "I could give you a brand-new face with it."

I tried but could not reconcile this steel-fisted father with the one I knew. This is the power of the drink: it can split a man into two different people, each a stranger to the other. The father I knew had never even lifted a hand to beat us, as if to do so were beneath him. His voice was warning enough: rich and deep and hollow. After he died I tried to remake his sound by murmuring into a rolled-up newspaper, until my mother finally grabbed the tube and smacked me senseless.

You see, I was his favorite. One morning he took me to the field and taught me how to guess that season's yield: eye a square meter, count the plants, then take the average beads of rice per plant. It was only a guess, he said, for to farm was to surrender control, to suspect but never know. We used maths and omens and traced our fortunes among the stars but—he shrugged—"Some signs are misleading. And none are any use to you."

"Why not?"

"You will grow into something greater than a farmer, my boy. Sure as calves become cows."

There was such magic to his words, the way he pressed a finger like a wand to my chest.

Jayan, meanwhile, had his own aspirations. He helped on the farm from time to time but mostly retreated to some shady corner of town with his friends, strays and idlers we never met.

Raghu had spied my brother with a rough bunch at a shappe, trading Tamil over toddy and fish. I said nothing of this to my mother, who would have thrown a great thumping fit on account of the fish eating.

As for me I much preferred spending my school-free hours with Raghu on his father's farm. Raghu's father was day to my father's night, two years older and temptation-proof. We called him Synthetic Achan (though not within earshot) due to his constant refrain: "Cola? What do you want to drink cola for? Cola is *crawling* with synthetics." The same went for boxed juices, white sugar, candies, chocolate, and most every other good and delicious thing.

And yet I loved Synthetic Achan, for he was the same man every hour of every day, begun with a glass of warm milk and finished off with a thimble of toddy and two smacks of the tongue. (Toddy was the only spirit he would touch, as it came straight from the coconut.) He was careful with his money and his land, having inherited seven acres to my father's six. At the end of each harvest he was rewarded with mountains of fragrant, golden, unmilled rice, which he stored in the shed. As children, Raghu and I would scramble up the mounds and slide down the sides until our legs itched from the husks. Itchy or not, this was the best time of my life.

But mine was a flimsy happiness, not the kind of happy that lasts.

The trouble began when my mother found a pouch of bullets in Jayan's cabinet—thick and crude as if sawed from a steering rod—and thrust the pouch at my father. She felt it a father's duty to straighten out a wayward son even if the father himself was wayward past hope.

That evening Jayan found my father waiting on the sit-out, sober for once. My mother and I hovered in the doorway.

"What are these for?" my father said, tossing the pouch of bullets at Jayan's feet.

Jayan took his time adjusting the new watch around his wrist before bending to pocket the bullets. The watch was a Solex, poor cousin to the Rolex, but gold and fine all the same. "For making money."

"Black money."

"Least it's mine."

My mother gripped the doorway, all the heat gone from her voice. "Not here. Inside."

But my father was already sailing down the steps on a wave of interrogation: Was it Jayan who had brought the gun into the house and was it Jayan who had been butchering elephants and God knew what else and was it Jayan who had so shamed his mother and father by becoming the one thing they had never dreamed he would be, a lowlife poacher, and in doing so, made them lowlives as well? Was it? Did Jayan have nothing to say for himself? Did he have a banana in his mouth?

Never before had my father spent so much breath on my brother. They had always been two lone wolves content to prowl their own sides of the mountain. Now Jayan's lips trembled as if in fear or remorse, I could not tell.

Then he broke out laughing.

"Shamed you?" said Jayan. "Shamed *you*?"

"Stop laughing."

"I used to think you were unlucky. Now I know you're just stupid."

In one swipe my father had him on the ground.

My mother ran to Jayan's side, but he blocked her with his arm. His watch face caught a glimpse of moonlight. It looked suddenly huge to me, so wrong on his slim wrist.

For a terrible second, I thought Jayan would charge at my father. Instead my brother dealt a blow much worse: he looked at my father and said we all wished him dead.

The thought had crossed my own mind once or twice. Indeed

I had imagined a fatherless life. Wouldn't you, if you watched your father day by day destroy your mother and drink away your land, wouldn't you once or twice imagine him resting in peace so you could honor what good memory of him remained and preserve what land and love were left?

Still Jayan should not have said it. To hear that truth out loud—it was a whipcrack to my heart.

My father tried to hide his hurt by spitting off to the side. But for a narrow moment his eyes met mine, and I saw the depths behind them, I saw how tired he was. Some men cannot master their many selves. My father was such a man, and he knew this just as he knew where his life would end.

One month later his body was pulled from a river. Bruises round the throat, a clump of his woolly beard torn out. My mother forbade us from speaking to the police for fear of reprisal, yet I could not rid the image from my mind—my father floating facedown on the water, all his hopes for me somewhere at the bottom.

Later I asked my brother, "You don't miss him at all?"

Jayan considered the question for less than a second. "Do you miss having a car?"

"We never had a car."

"That we did not."

Jayan worked in the field till the sun striped his arms, till dirt gummed his nails and streaked his legs from standing calf-deep in mud. He followed my father's right-hand man on morning rounds, learning how to sow seeds and replant the shoots stalk by tender stalk, to read the crop by its color and posture, when to feed nitrogen to sallow plants, when to set out magnesium cakes for the rats who sucked the juice from the base of a broken stalk. Whether by mistake or misfortune or a savage flock of doves, the first two plantings suffered. In the meantime, my brother kept up his side business.

He learned to read the crop, and I learned to read him. The day before a hunt, he was always glancing at the trees, listening for his omen, the woodpecker. If the woodpecker called from the east, I would glimpse my brother the next morning slipping past the house in his hunting uniform—green half pant and black T-shirt. If, the day after he returned from the forest, a blue Maruti drove up to the shed and my brother stuffed a fertilizer sack in the trunk, the hunt had gone well. If the driver haggled with my brother at length, Jayan would assume a foul mood for the rest of the day.

As a new policy my mother turned her gaze elsewhere, for she believed Jayan might abandon us forever if pressed too hard. I never shared her doubt, yet Jayan was Jayan, and he had his days. Some nights he drank with his feckless friends, and as the hours went on, he turned his frustrations onto the nearest bystander and came home fat lipped and dented. Easy to forget he was but twenty years old.

On hunts, I would come to learn, Jayan led a gang of four. Among them he was the gunman, making twice as much as the others who carried supplies. He was careful to keep these associates apart from me out of embarrassment. He said I was fragile as a flower when it came to physical tasks, a theory he based on my love of books. (He rarely read anything longer than a receipt.)

So I was unpleasantly surprised when Jayan invited Raghu and me on a business trip to Kottayam. Jayan would be meeting with his boss, a man by the name of Communist Chacko, with whom he hoped to deal directly instead of haggling with that driver over every ounce of ivory.

"Why can't you ask one of your other colleagues?" I said. "That one fat-necked fellow you're always running with."

"I cannot trust him for a thing like this, and I cannot go alone, I'll look like a nobody."

"But we have school."

"We can skip it," Raghu volunteered. This was Raghu—quick to answer even if no one had asked him a question. He was eager for adventure and adulthood, a moment of glory in his otherwise inglorious life. He was also eager to skip class.

"Good," said Jayan, and to me: "We will save you a seat."

By "seat," he meant a sliver of space in a mini-lorry that pummeled my hind parts for most of the five-hour journey. All throughout Raghu asked questions about hunting and guns as if studying for a job interview. Jayan told of the time he went for a five-day hunt and found himself having to eat a dinner of boiled black monkey. "I begged them to cut off the head before cooking it, but they said the brain was the best part." Jayan shook his head. "All curled up and tail cut. Looked just like a baby boiling in a pot."

Not a second too soon we reached Communist Chacko's house, a stucco hulk with stone dolphins on the gateposts. Raghu thought it all folly and waste ("What is the point? A house can't feed a man"), but Jayan told him to shut up and say nothing until we were back on the road.

Communist Chacko had been trained as a lawyer—he always attached "Esq." to the tail of his signature—but he was the picture of a politician with that smile, as slick and white as his marble floor. Framed photos claimed every wall, his sons Lenin and Stalin featured in most. The boys were poor in school but no matter, said Communist Chacko, Lenin-Stalin would follow him into the family business. Names like theirs they wouldn't find a job that easy. The names had been Dolly's idea. His wife's people were total Marxists. Communist Chacko didn't mind. "You know the best part of being a Marxist? You don't have to go to church." For one who never went to church, the man liked to preach.

Communist Chacko led us out the back door, bypassing a shed that hummed with machinery. At the foot of a steep metal staircase, he kicked up his mundu and squinted at the summit. "Come. The birds are waiting."

What the hell kind of code was he speaking? Were "the birds" his associates awaiting us in that tarp-lined chamber on the roof? I was the last to clang up the wobbly rungs and emerge into a small space that contained Communist Chacko, Jayan, Raghu, and seven wire cages of fowl.

There were two to each cage, husband and wife, most of them feathered in red, yellow, and green. Communist Chacko puckered his lips at a nearby parrot, who clung to the wire with dainty taloned feet. He raised a fingertip to its beak; the parrot bit gently and released. "She's a sweet one," said Communist Chacko. "The others will snip your switch off."

"What are they for?" Raghu whispered to me.

"Breeding and selling," said Communist Chacko. "You should see the cockatoos mate, it's quite charming."

I would have sooner watched a dog make turds, but in the spirit of pleasing our host, I peered into a cage of small parakeets. Four whites and two grays flicked their necks this way and that.

"I had a macaw," Communist Chacko said wistfully. "He flew off. Can you imagine—watching one whole lakh dissolve into blue sky?"

"Maybe not a whole lakh," said my brother. "But I know what it is to lose hard-earned money."

Communist Chacko grinned at one of the switch-snippers. "You had a falling-out with Babu."

"He takes too great a cut and for what? For his car? We have a mini-lorry."

"Yes, I saw. Not the most inconspicuous vehicle." The fat man gazed into another cage, where a diseased-looking parakeet perched alone, ragged and balding in patches, eyes like milky bulging marbles. It held itself perfectly still, wings folded tight around a tortured heart.

"He is inconsistent," my brother went on. "Haggling like a fishmonger, wasting my time. And who is he to judge the grade? The man has cataracts for god's sake."

Communist Chacko sighed as if all this backbiting were undignified. His breath ruffled the blind bird's breast.

"Will it die?" I asked, forgetting my brother's no-talk policy. He gave me a look that said he would bury me in my books.

"Fairly soon I would think," said Communist Chacko. "Do you like animals?"

"None I would like to see mating."

Communist Chacko laughed. "I am not a sentimental person, you know. If you told me tomorrow their feathers were precious in China, I would be out here plucking the lovelies myself."

Communist Chacko stepped back from the cages and resumed his preacher voice: "And God said unto Man, Be fruitful and multiply and have dominion over the fish of the sea and over the fowl of the air and over every living thing that moves upon the earth." Raghu nodded along like a born-again.

"OK, do this," said Communist Chacko. "Deliver the tusks directly to me. I will give you two thousand more per kilo. But this is on a one-month trial basis only. Any little problem and we go back to the old way."

After taking specific directions on protocol—where to drop off and when and to whom—we left the preacher to his fowl and emerged into the swollen heat. I trotted down the last few steps, somehow uplifted by my brother's success and my hand in it. And perhaps I would have forgotten all about the shed had it not shrieked at me as I passed. My brother and cousin walked ahead, unhearing. The door was ajar.

How well I recall the world in that narrow room. Two long tables covered in a forest of white figurines. A troop of tiny elephants. Bangles smooth and stacked. And in the far corner a giant Nataraj with one sleek limb raised, all in ivory.

Several craftsmen sat at the tables, some carving with awls fine as a sparrow's claw. A man ground a piece against a whetstone. A young boy went from table to table, using a careful cupped hand to sweep ivory shavings into a bag.

"We sell them to Ayurvedic doctors," Communist Chacko said, causing my heart to jump. "Little ivory powder and coconut oil could do wonders for your dandruff."

"I do not have dandruff."

"Then I suppose that shit on your shoulder is snow."

As I brushed at my shirt, I could feel his eyes on me, narrowing.

"You are a curious fellow, aren't you?" he said.

"Sorry, sir, the door was open—"

"Oh, I don't care. I have a license. Got it ten years before the ban, luckily."

"So the Forest Department looks the other way?"

"Depends on who is doing the looking." He pointed to a pair of tusks on a nearby table. "Those are for P. K. Kurian, the divisional range officer before that lardy little Muslim took over. She's a tough one. Have you met her?"

"No."

Communist Chacko ushered me out of the shed, closing the door. "Count yourself lucky."

So every other month Jayan and his fat-necked associate drove their spoils to Kottayam and I returned to my studies quite happily. I was only fifteen years old, yet I had mapped the course of my life—to do my pre-degree in Commerce and attend college and someday be chief manager of a bank, with my own glass-walled office where visitors had to wait their turn. Jayan may have been our lifeboat in those days, but I would build a great ship of myself. I would keep the sea so calm my mother would hardly feel it shift beneath her feet.

But ships take a long time to build, much longer than it takes to build a dream. In the meantime Jayan would give her no peace.

One dull gray morning, the mini-lorry came up the road and stopped before our house. My brother stepped out, followed by a woman who kept her apologetic gaze on the ground.

She had dainty toe rings on each of her dusty feet, the sort of ornament that seemed to me both ridiculous and intriguing. I tried not to look too hard at her face, at the lashes that grazed her cheeks. I tried to appear calm when Jayan introduced her as his wife. Leela. A woman he had found and then married in a Kottayam courthouse.

Oh, the fit my mother threw. How could Jayan do such a thing? Elope with some Christian no-name without even a hello-goodbye to his mother? What kind of loose shameless beef-eating she-dog would run off with a Hindu, no engagement, no dowry, no nothing? (The indecent kind, that's what—the taking-advantage kind!) And why did Jayan think the beef-eater would never run from him?

From the look of her, Leela seemed the kind of woman who had been fed an exclusive diet of pomegranate and almonds and milk, by which I mean she was fair and softly built, her features made to fill a movie screen. "World class, mangoes like that." Raghu sighed. I smacked his head. He smacked me back, claiming she wasn't *his* sister.

Leela had lived her life on the coast and had never seen the forests and valleys and ghats my brother had promised her. Once she asked me: "Is it true the tribals are so dark because they are partway African?"

"Partway who?"

She toyed with the tip of her braid. "I heard the tribals married the African slaves that the Britishers brought with them. That is why the tribals are so dark. Because of the Africans." Hesitantly she added, "There are no tribals in my village."

I stared at her, much conflicted with thoughts. *You are simple and silly. You are the most beautiful thing I have seen. You are married to my brother. Why? My brother has the brain of a wall lizard. I am sharp in school. I am sure to make something of myself, sure as calves become cows. But will Mother let me find a Leela of my own? No. Because every family only allows itself one mistake. You are that beautiful mistake. And now I will marry some cross-eyed callus-hoofed heifer with whom my stars align.*

"Not because of the Africans," she concluded, a blush warming her cheeks.

All the facts we knew of Leela could have fit on the side of a toothpaste box. Her people hailed from some flyspeck village she neglected to name. She had no schooling or training. Her father was a bricklayer. How she and Jayan had met was a mystery my mother titled Their Filthy Beginnings and refused to read a single page.

If the world according to my mother was out of joint, the crop showed no sign of it. The stalks were growing strong, nodding strands of rice fine as seed pearls. Leela survived my mother's silence behind a wall of politeness, swift to melt out of sight if my mother was in a mood. No sooner had my mother finished her morning tea than Leela whisked the cup away to rinse it. She took up the washing and ironing and sweeping while my mother pointed out every stain and crinkle and crumb, as if she had personally invented the art of housewifery.

All this abuse Leela bore with a steady temper. Jayan's puppy love seemed sustenance enough. She basked in his stinky presence whenever he returned from the fields, and he was no less infatuated, his hand always grasping her waist, her braid, her bottom, handful upon handful and never enough. He only took such liberties at what he presumed were private moments, but in a three-room house few moments are private.

Sometimes I heard the tight murmur of an argument through the walls, likely to do with his continued visits to the forest. The wild was always reaching for Jayan, noisy and glowing with adventure. No matter how they fought, she always stood by the door in the sullen dawn and watched him leave for the fields.

"I worry about him," she said to me once, after Jayan had gone away.

Get used to it, I thought.

"He says there is no reason to worry. What's so wrong with cutting a tree, he says. But there must be something wrong if there are laws against it."

"What tree?" I asked.

"Sandalwood. His side business. Isn't it?"

I stared directly into those simple eyes. My silence made the answer plain, did it not? Yet I could not betray my brother completely; I could give no further answer than this: "Ask him."

She hadn't the chance to take my advice, for the day Jayan returned from his final trip, he was all *Later later not now.* The day passed without the mini-lorry coming up the road, and by noon the next day my brother was in a black mood. I knew what had him pacing—there was ivory in the shed, the marrow drying, the weight lightening, the price lessening with every passing gram.

By dusk my brother secured a car for the following morning and vowed never to work with that irresponsible bastard ever again. Little did he know the bastard had already taken the same vows.

For that very night the Karnataka police punched at our door and clomped through our sitting room and took my brother from his bed before he had a shirt on his back. They yapped a mix of Kannada and Malayalam, something about crossing state lines with weapons. They retrieved the ivory from the shed, piece after piece wrapped in newspaper and nested like eggs in the cauldron never to hatch a penny. By the time Leela went running out into the yard with a blue mundu, the policemen were leading my brother to the jeep.

See the spectacle of us standing outside our house in the night. Leela holding a blue mundu. My mother shouting at the police. Me at fifteen, watching my brother in nothing but his chaddi between two brutes who have not the decency to let him put on a shirt.

It is difficult to place faith in a man who tells you during a ten-minute phone call from prison not to worry. But Jayan convinced us that Communist Chacko would post bail as he had done twice before. "Twice? What twice?" demanded Leela. My brother said he had no time to explain. He promised there would be no trial.

But Communist Chacko failed to provide bail on account of my brother's previous debts, which I suspected were to do with those previous bonds. And so the trial would go on. Old fat-neck would play witness for the prosecution.

Their relations had curdled of late, ever since the fat-neck had demanded his turn at the gun and the doubled wage that went with it. My brother felt he could not be trusted, neither with his aim nor with the splitting of the money, another task that fell to the gunman. So Jayan refused him, and the traitor went straight to the police to feed them a fable about his U-turn of heart and his fresh respect for the law. Judge and jury would fall upon the fairy tale like crows on a carcass.

Whereas once my brother had won praise for being a perfect shot, now he was cast out by public opinion. Rumors ran loose that he had made big money off elephant game—why else had the Karnataka police crossed their border to collect him? Most everyone, Christian and Muslim and Hindu alike, believed killing elephants for money was a sinful pursuit, and worse that he should profit from it, hoarding untold sums, when everyone else accepted whatever skinny salary this life afforded them.

"What money!" Leela railed at me, as if I stood in for all of society. "He shot four or five elephants, that is all. He swore to me. How can they lock him away on account of four elephants?"

Okay fine, I let her believe it was four. I told myself this was not my business but theirs. Here is the truth: I would have sworn nonsense on her King James Bible if only to prevent her from leaving us, leaving me.

Most strenuously, my brother insisted that there was no need for us to come to the trial in Karnataka. Surely the jury would deem the fat-neck a faulty witness on account of his record, blotted by the petty felonies of an idiot. (Once, he attempted to burgle an office building and got himself locked in the entry.) It was too far to travel for a case that would be over in minutes. And if we were to come, who would mind the farm?

Jayan knew—how could he not, with his front-row seat—that the magistrate court would find him guilty. His was a sorry gift, the one and only he could give: an excuse not to see him with his slim wrists in the irons, to continue our days as if nothing were different.

Four years my brother was gone from us. My mother spent most of this time confined to the house, held hostage by the belief that gawkers and gossips were waiting outside our door, their whispers burrowing through the walls. A bad husband was a misfortune. A bad son was her fault, and she felt she deserved every word said against her.

Regarding gossips, Leela said there was no use listening to every twit with a mouth. She knotted a cloth around her head, picked up a sickle, and labored in the fields alongside the adiya women who eyed the way she whacked at the stalks, sweating, cursing, cutting nothing. Eventually they showed her how to sharpen the blade against bamboo, then shear. She found the money to buy chickens and a cow named White Girl, earning us income from the eggs and milk. The chicks she guarded as fiercely as if she had laid them herself, but the predators were many. One day a vulture whisked a chick in its claws but lost its grip upon takeoff. Belly up, the chick lay cheeping in the dirt, a glistening string of its innards plucked out. Finished, I thought, and all the eggs it would have laid for us.

But Leela did not waste a second in telling me to bring needle and thread. I had threaded her many a needle by then, but never had I seen her do what she did: carefully cradling the chick in her palm and fingering the innards back inside as if stuffing a pastry puff. Like a surgeon, she stitched the belly whole again, then patted a paste of turmeric over the wound.

In the end that stitched-up chicken outlived the others. It even followed her around like some lovesick suitor who would not take no for an answer, a behavior I might have found humorous if it did not so closely resemble my own frame of mind.

Yet I was not her only fan, so to speak.

Two fellows called me out of the house one day, asking for Podimattom Leela. One had a long face, lizardy features. He said he knew her from before, that they were old friends. Business associates, said the other, a fellow with a face all wrinkled and scarred like a halved head of cabbage. They had heard about her financial trouble. They thought they could help.

The lizard smiled with tiny teeth. She can find us at Hotel Meriya, he said and left.

I found Leela out back, standing over a massive jackfruit, one of the three Synthetic Achan had given us, knowing I favored the fried chips. She bit her lip as if angry with that spiny green boulder, its stem dribbling sap.

"Are they gone?" she asked.

I nodded. She handed me the hoe. I lifted the thing over my head and struck the fruit. I turned the jack by a degree, then hacked again. Turned it. Hacked. Turn. Hack.

She bent and used her fingers to pry the halves apart, the gluey sap fouling up her fingers. Each half displayed a daisy shape, with its pale yellow bulbs of fruit like petals around the pulpy core. With a kitchen knife she began carving the halves into quarters, still saying nothing, her mouth in a knot.

I asked why they had called her Podimattom Leela. She told me it was the place where she was born.

"No one calls me Sitamala Manu."

She was quiet.

"They said you were business associates," I said.

"Customers."

"What kind."

"Same kind as your brother." She spoke oh so casually, but I could see the tears sitting on the rims of her eyes. I felt a small mean wish to see them fall.

Instead she tossed the knife onto the newspaper and dipped her fingers in a steel cup of oil, rubbing the white from her fingers as she brushed past me.

I caught her by the arm. "I deserve to know . . ."

"Know what. Spit it out."

Heat filled my face. The question required finesse. I had no finesse. I had a hoe in my hand.

"All that honey talk about sandalwood trees . . ." She shook her head. "Don't talk to me about deserve."

I dropped my gaze. I could think of nothing to say.

After a while she spoke in a small voice. "Knowing those two, it will be all over town by tomorrow."

"It will not. I won't let them."

"Oho. My hero." She smirked at the mess of jackfruit at our feet. "Leave it, Manu, just leave it."

Another man would have let the moment pass and put the matter out of mind. But I was not a man; I was a boy of sixteen seething with impulse and anger, and I felt it my job to defend her. Raghu refused to join me, having seen the cretins and citing very bad odds.

I found the lizard at the shappe next door to Hotel Meriya,

holding court among his fellows, not a puddle's worth of sense among them. The lizard caught my approach out the corner of his eye and threw himself wholeheartedly into a one-man show. Podimattom Leela! Like a butcher he appraised her parts, tongue by breast by thigh, and oh the things she could do with certain of them. Her menu never changed, long and all-inclusive, nothing left off the list and believe you me her mouth never tired—

"Neither does yours."

The shiteater grinned at me. I kept my hands in the pockets of my brother's old trousers. "Ah. Here's her bodyguard."

"Leela Shivaram is her name."

"How was I supposed to know that? She didn't invite me to the wedding."

"Now you know."

"I knew her differently."

"You knew someone else."

He shrugged. "Wash a crow all you want, it won't turn white."

I asked him to step out. Lazily he sucked at a fish bone before heaving himself up from the table. It was difficult to maintain my air of aggression while he rinsed every mote from his mouth.

He followed me some ways from the shappe to a stand of trees, where I turned to find the cabbage head in attendance. My heart fell. "What is he for?"

"Not to referee, I can tell you that."

I kept my eyes on his feet while my fist grew hard in my pocket, four fingers looped in my father's steel. I remembered the knuckles dull and deadly in my brother's palm. The lizard asked if I wanted to rethink my opinions, to which I replied by smashing my metal fist into his snout.

He spun and landed face flat on the dirt, his arms spread in a pose that recalled my father, and for a terrible moment I thought he was dead.

The cabbage head stared at his colleague, who to my great relief struggled like a newborn to lift his head. In those few seconds of gawking, I had time enough to sling the knuckles into the trees so they wouldn't be used against me. My fingers rang with pain.

Take note: I did not run. Unlike my father, I knew not to rack up my debts.

The cabbage head sighed and gave me a look of almost fatherly disappointment. Then he popped me in the ear, the chin, and—with breathtaking finality—the belly.

Laid out on the grass, I braced for the final kick, one that would send me to deepest sleep, when from somewhere above came a voice: "Get off him or I will shoot you to pieces."

The world was rocking all around me, but I made out the shape of a boy holding a rifle. A boy whose chicken-bone arms looked much like the arms of Raghu.

"That gun's taller than you," said the cabbage head. "Probably not even loaded."

The young gunman leveled his barrel. "Take a bet, pussy man."

Oh, it was a first-class performance, so convincing that the cabbage head surrendered and carried his colleague away, tossing limp threats. Soon as they were gone, Raghu hustled me home, his utmost fear being that Synthetic Achan would discover that his gun had gone missing. The barrel was carved with rabbits—this much I remember of the rifle that I would meet later on, under darker circumstances. I also remember the glow of triumph in Raghu's face as we rode home in an auto.

"What took you so long," I mustered through the functioning side of my mouth. "One more punch and they would have pulped me."

"Look in the mirror, little boy—you are pulped."

"I got one of them good."

"Now you're hallucinating."

And on like that we quipped and quarreled, in place of a gratitude I knew not how to give.

I spent the next days in a fog of pain. In letters I mentioned none of this to Jayan. It was an unspoken rule that our letters should contain nothing but peaceful scenes, a home sweeter than the home he remembered.

For us he painted prison in similar shades:

At 6 we get chai in our cells. At 630 we go into compound and you can play chess or carrom or read the paper. I read the paper. There are 3 std phone booths. Nice library. One man here for 15 years he got his LLB and two other degrees in jail. I would school myself in the law if I did not hate all lawyers so much. I could get better advice from the ceiling.

None of us believed that jail was the luxury law school of Jayan's description. Still we were most unprepared for our maiden visit.

In the week prior, my mother and Leela had built a feast that would fill my brother's belly ten times over, with jars of achar, both lemon and mango, and sambar and avial and rice. Half of it spoiled in the heat while we waited to obtain security clearance. Three hours of standing for thirty minutes of staring through a metal web so thick our hands could not touch his. I finally understood why he had kept us from coming so long. To see him in this state made my mother lose her speech.

For he was someone else, my brother, eyes bulgy as a drunk's, collarbones so high you could snap them like pencils. Even his manner of speech had changed, rambling on and on so as to leave no room for response. All he wished to discuss was the barbarity and indecency of the Karnataka justice system. In Karnataka, 30 percent of the inmates were innocent. In Karnataka, if a man killed himself, his wife was arrested as an accessory. In Karnataka, you could get six months for smoking.

Fat lot of good to claim innocence when the whole of Karnataka begged to differ. Of course my mother and Leela said no such thing, nor did I. Mostly we kept our commentary to *How are you?* and *What can we bring you?* We well knew the answers, but there was such yearning in those thirty minutes, such blind desperation as the time ran dry.

At one point he turned his red eyes on me. "What happened to your nose?"

"Nothing." My hand went to my nose, where a welt remained from last month's bout. "I punched someone."

"*You?*"

"Why not me?"

"Over what?"

Leela pierced me with a look. I had lied to both her and my mother, but one glance at my ramshackle face, and Leela had known.

"Mugged." My mother sighed. "Can you imagine? In the broad light of day."

As the years went by, we drew hope from whatever lightless

corner we could. When the newspapers told that Karnataka would pardon a lotteried pick of prisoners on November 1, in celebration of the state birthday, we waited for lots that were never drawn. When Jayan dismissed his lawyer, we hired another, but they were mosquitoes, those people, always buzzing in your ear and at the same time bleeding you dry.

By the time Jayan was freed, I was a young man of nineteen, my hopes for college on hold. I had told myself I would pursue my degree as soon as Jayan came home, but I had not foreseen what captivity could do to a man over the course of four years.

All his swagger and ease had worn off. He had a guarded look about him, the flinch of a hunted thing. He slept all day and smoked all night, as if to make up for the bidis he could not buy in prison. He was both familiar and strange to us, as we must have been to him.

I avoided my brother, but the women handled him more delicately. My mother moved around him with care, and Leela rushed to his side if he so much as belched, as though he were a spill about to run off the table's edge. She tacked his name to the end of every sentence as if to remind him of it.

One night I heard him talking to Leela in a voice mean and muttery. She wanted him to go with her to temple for the Sita Devi Festival, the grandest hullabaloo for miles, but Jayan was in no mood. "I might as well have THIEF tattooed on my forehead, that is how everyone looks at me."

"So let them look. We have nothing to hide now. All the time you were gone I kept my chin up. I worked. I bent my knee for no one."

"Who gave you the cow and the chickens?"

"I bought them."

"With what money?"

She paused. "My wedding chain."

A long, vast silence.

"You should have left," he said.

"And go where? Who would have me?"

"Your sisters."

"They would have my money but they would not have me."
A muttering from Jayan. "You know why. And anyway, they can't
give me children."

I heard my brother carefully clear his throat.

"I am tired of waiting," she said. "You promised me a life."

Jayan said nothing. Her voice shifted to a different key, all
soft and wanting as she asked, *Should I be more specific?* . . .
thus leading to the sort of commentary that robbed me of
sleep.

As the months sped on, Jayan seemed to grow into a sturdier self.
He resumed his work in the fields, and I often went with him,
leaving Raghu behind. Even when Raghu invited me to watch
Junior Mandrake at his house, on their brand-new LG TV, I said
I was tired, having worked beside Jayan all day, Jayan who never
tired or paused for a drink.

"But it's starring Jagathy," Raghu said. "You like Jagathy."

"I like my bed better."

Raghu rubbed one skinny foot with the other. "You never help
out at our place anymore."

"You already have enough help."

"Well, Father says you have to sit in the palli with me tonight."

"Tonight? I'm too tired."

"Not too tired for that pumpkin of yours." He raised his voice loud enough for my mother to hear. "What's her name—Kamini? Yamini?"

I told him to go screw a stone.

To be clear: I did not know "screw a stone" would be my final words to Raghu, my cousin-brother and truest friend, who had saved my life not long before he lost his own. It gnaws at me still that I did not go to meet him that night, but the worst thing I did was to witness the hurt in his face and walk away.

§

Six months after my brother was released, my cousin was killed.

In the days after his death, Raghu appeared at temple and in the fields and one time on the back of a lorry. I had been similarly visited by my father for a while. I once chased a public bus, sure I had seen my father inside taking the tickets.

Work was the only wall I could lean against. Given my mother's permission, I took to toiling in Synthetic Achan's fields, as he was short a pair of hands. Not that my uncle wanted mine. He abominated my very presence and would not glance my way, not even when he uttered an order, not even when I said, at the end of the day, "I'll go and come," to which he issued not even a grunt. I poured my sweat into his soil and came up with a possible solution for the parakeets that came cackling out of the sky and into the rice. One whole morning I spent staking two poles along the eastern side of his farm and twisting a long length of white plastic between them, strung with bottle caps and bells. The plastic flashed and glimmered, jangling in the breeze. My uncle asked if I was scaring the little shits or throwing them a party.

At night I lay awake thinking of the Gravedigger, a name I had known since childhood along with its other titles. Schoolchildren had set its killing spree to song:

> *Here it comes*
> *the Ottayan, the Undertaker*
> *Sent its master*
> *to his Maker*

What had that master done, I wondered, to give his elephant such a fiending for death?

In the days that followed, the Gravedigger took one more palli and one more soul. The palli belonged to a farm down the way, its walls crashed to kindling. The man inside escaped and lived to feed us a dubious story: *I was lying on my side by the fire lost in a daydream when I felt a sniff at my ear so gentle I half thought it was my wife, though, honestly speaking, she would sooner fart in church than show affections, so I turned and found myself faced with the Gravedigger's big fat hose! I did not think, I drew back my fist and punched it—dsh!—in the nostrils. Naturally it was not expecting such heroics, for it snatched its trunk away, giving me just enough time to jump out and run.*

We could not question the Kuruva woman. She had been hauling firewood on her back, skirting the forest, when the Gravedigger found her. Dozens of women had likely done the same to keep their cook fires burning, each convinced that *she* would not be the one to cross the murderer's path. A whole morning passed before a lorry slowed and noticed a little cushion of a foot jutting from beneath piled wood. As in the case of my cousin, the Gravedigger had conducted its own private burial.

And so, the Forest Department cautioned us with the obvious: to keep to our homes at dusk. It promoted the Gravedigger to rogue status but stopped short of issuing the order for its killing. Not until it would kill more of our own.

In the meantime I kept to Synthetic Achan's fields. I woke at 6:00 a.m., several hours before the laborers came fresh off the jeep. This was a tough half-lazy lot of men who demanded a thimble or two of Old Cask for breakfast. When they cut, I cut, and when they heaved bundles on their heads, so did I.

In the evenings I lingered in my uncle's fields. From the rear of his house I watched the rose-orange sky and the goats among the balsa blooms and the mountains beyond, hiding the Gravedigger in their deeps.

Before long the parakeets interrupted my idyll, sailing triumphantly over my slack piece of plastic. Down they swooped in a green flittering cloud and clipped the beaded strands before lifting away. My sole defense was to hoot and bang a spoon against a tin pan, but the pretty thieves had already fled for the trees, where they would pick at the rice just as crows pick at a dead man's eyes.

The parakeets were unusually quiet when Synthetic Achan came up beside me. "Your little ribbon didn't work."

"There's not enough wind."

"I don't care about the birds," he said. "I have a bigger problem."

I snuck a glance across his face and wondered when the hair at his temples had gone gray.

"Guess who came to pay respects," he said. "Forest Department."

"When?"

"Some days ago. They said they would give me ten thousand rupees for damages, so long as I filled out some form. 'An Application for Compensation,' they called it. The pigs. I said, *What should I do with it? Buy another son?* But then I had an idea." He turned to me. "I could give it to you and Jayan."

"You don't owe us anything."

"I know that. It's you who owes me."

How smooth and cold the claim. How heavy the hand on my shoulder.

"You want us to kill the Gravedigger?"

"Louder, boy, the greenbacks didn't hear you."

I shook my head. "Jayan will say no. He will not go to jail again."

"Just listen. Your brother made the mistake of working with some no-name ruffian. This time we are all on Jayan's side, all us farmers. No one would fault him or name him to the police." I had trouble picturing this second family of farmers—where had they been for the past four years? "All our people want some safety for our fields, our harvest, our children . . ."

Am I not your child? I wanted to ask. But the mere mention of children had stolen his voice. He turned away and repeatedly rubbed his nose with his finger as if to give his face something to do.

"If they accuse your brother or you or anyone else, I will confess to it. I will stand trial; I will take it all on my head, I swear it. No difference between living out here and living in a cage." He paused and added softly, "Not to me."

He had never looked so old, and yet in his ruined face I saw an echo of my cousin.

"He listens to you, Manu."

I stood in silence, yet what choice did I have? I look back at the young man I was and see a boy, powerless before the only person he had yearned all his life to call Father.

I tried to approach my brother, but it was impossible to find him alone what with his wife around every corner. Leela put no trust in Jayan and kept one ear always tilted in his direction lest he should slip into his old ways. A pretty warden she made, but a warden all the same.

At last I found him in the courtyard. He was raking a fat pile of harvest, forking and fluffing the stalks, sweating as he went. In two more days the stalks would dry and he would steer the cattle-drawn plow around the pile, threshing the rice to loosen the hulls.

All I desired was a pause to precede our discussion, but Jayan kept talking as if to avoid it. That day his chosen subject was the tractor-tiller. "Kunjappen said the tractor-tiller can do in thirty minutes what the plow takes hours to do."

"We used his contraption last year. More bugs in that rice than lice on a stray."

"What is that to do with the tractor-tiller?"

Back and forth we bickered on the merits and follies of the tractor-tiller until I blurted, "I talked to Synthetic Achan."

"Talking now, is he?"

I relayed Synthetic Achan's request. Jayan listened in silence, doing more stabbing than fluffing.

"How much is he offering?" Jayan said finally.

"Ten thousand at the least."

"And he wants me to do it."

"Not you," I said quickly. "We thought you would know someone else for the job."

"Someone eager to go to jail? There's a rare species."

"No one would go to jail. Uncle swore it."

"Who made him chief minister?"

"He watched over us while you were gone."

"And for that I give him my thanks. But not the rest of my life."

A fair answer, I admit. Jayan simply wanted to make an honest living, upright and in the open. I wanted a cure for my guilt.

As if guessing my thoughts, Jayan said, "Raghu is dead. And if you had been with him that night, you would be too."

"You don't know that."

"I do know that. You run like an old woman."

He gave a demonstration, amusing only himself.

"What do I tell Synthetic Achan?"

"Tell him you have other duties now." A smile tugged at his mouth. "Tell him you will soon be an uncle yourself."

Hard to believe I had not realized Leela was five months pregnant. Indeed I had noticed she was plumping in places, but I had assumed she was gaining weight the way many young wives pack their middles and behinds, trading their slim-waisted skirts for house gowns.

After Jayan disclosed her secret, I could notice nothing else. Though Leela had barely a bump beneath her house gown, suddenly it seemed to me that her attributes were growing by the minute. Twice she caught my ungallant eye and began a habit of tossing a towel over her bosom whenever I approached with a glass of warm milk or a boiled egg or whatever my mother had me bring her.

Intent on building a life of substance for his child, Jayan worked long days, drank much less, and even took Leela to temple for some baby-blessing ceremony. He enlisted my help in digging a trench around the shed where we kept our rice bureau locked. Other farmers had reported elephant raids to their sheds, where a single beast could sniff out and swallow a year's worth of food. We hired a few more hands to help with the digging and bolstered the side walls with timber. Over it we laid down a plank for crossing.

My mother filed many a complaint against the plank, but my brother thought it the only solution. What would she have him do—plant a bitter hedge around the shed like Kunjappen had done? One bull had braved the taste, then suffered loose motions all over the walls and bushes.

Speaking of smells, I suppose the outhouse is not a topic of dignified discourse, but let me indulge because as you will see the toilet and its placement would alter the course of our lives.

When Jayan was in jail, Synthetic Achan undertook renovations on his house and offered a few to ours, partly out of generosity and also out of shame that his own brother's family should still be living under a paddy-grass roof. My mother installed a gas stove, which she never used unless guests were in the house; she much preferred the smoky infusions of a wood-burning stove. She had the paddy-grass roof switched to tile. I missed the look of the grass when it was fresh and sun dazzled, but I did not miss the way it grizzled and grayed over the months until we had to haul fresh grass onto the frame.

The single modernity my mother would not accept was a toilet inside the house. "But no one has an outhouse anymore," I told her. "Ours is an inconvenience."

"What," she said, "to take ten steps outside for your business?" Neither Leela nor I could persuade my mother. She plainly refused to suffer the sounds and smells and squalor of a toilet spreading through our rooms.

Now that Leela was pregnant, my mother regretted her prior stance. She had not considered the burdens of pregnancy, one being that every ten minutes the pregnant woman is on her way to do the needful. In the middle of the night Leela would slip out without turning on a light. Between the churning notes of Jayan's snore, I listened for her footsteps to make sure she had not fallen.

On a night such as this, her footsteps fading, I drifted off and later awoke to the hushed hiss of rain.

I peeked into my brother's room. Her side of the mattress lay empty. I shook him until he turned and saw her gone, the scowl fading from his face.

Without waking my mother, we rushed into the drizzle. I had to feel my way along the clothesline strung between our back door and the outhouse, which kept us from straying on moonless nights. The outhouse door lay ajar. Empty.

"Manu," he said, staring at the banana tree cracked in half, its crown in the dirt. Our fishtail palm shorn of two huge fans. I knelt over a rounded depression of earth, my eyes leaping to the next and the next where they all at once disappeared as if the elephant had taken flight.

Hoarsely, my brother shouted her name. Soon my mother came running around the house wielding a flashlight. We searched and we searched. The sky was dark and wild, trees writhing in the wind. A calm took me over. I called her name as if she were nearby, not gored or mashed or tangled in the branches of a tree. I looked, but all I could see was Raghu's palli in splinters before me.

At last my mother shouted us over to the trench that surrounded the rice shed. She was kneeling at the edge.

There lay Leela on her back, her nightie twisted up around her soiled knees. The flashlight glared upon her face, but she lay still and pretty as a battered doll in the trench we had dug deep as a grave.

Imagine her on that moonless night. She has just done her needful when she hears the splintering of timber. Dread steps softly up her spine. She stands up slow on trembling knees and, for a moment, nothing moves. She wills herself to unhook the rusty latch and exit the outhouse.

There it is waiting, like a suitor come calling.

The Gravedigger nods, its trunk upcurled, and lets out a breath. Raindrops slither around her bare neck, but she feels nothing. Is it panting? Is it a vision? She feels far away, a phantom among the living.

Her heart thuds in her throat, a reminder of what she is: flesh and marrow, spit and vigor. Mother-to-be.

How she runs.

Blood pounds in her ears louder than the Gravedigger's feet, but its stride is long and impossible. They are two animals locked in the ancient dance of hunter and hunted, and a small part of her considers one possible end—her end—just as the earth consumes her.

The Elephant

The flames of tiny lamplights trembled down the road to the temple. The Gravedigger could smell the hot oil, the chili-rubbed corn, the ice cream and peanuts, the plastic of inflatable toys, the petals of flowers, marigolds and rose water, all these shifting, rippling scents, and beneath them all, a heavy silt: the smell of people.

The Gravedigger was new to the festival season, new to parading and blessing and standing in wait. Seven months before, at the Sanctuary, he had been visited by a man who fed him a handful of caramels. Nosing through the man's pockets, the Gravedigger found more. Old Man spoke sharply, but the Candy Man laughed and spread his arms, his knuckles stroking the underside of the Gravedigger's trunk. His eyes were small and set deep, like seeds.

So one day the Gravedigger was picking the Candy Man's pockets; the next day he was trapped in an open truck bed and bumping down the road to a new home. Sudden changes disagreed with the Gravedigger. He still trembled when remembering the day he was trucked out of the forest and into the Sanctuary, when life narrowed to a pitch-black cavern, and every which way was a wall. Then, as now, he perceived little of his situation. One comfort sustained him—that Old Man had come along.

· · ·

The Gravedigger did not understand that he had been purchased by the Candy Man, who was locally known as Elephant Sabu. In addition to the Gravedigger, Elephant Sabu owned seven elephants, six of which he rented out for logging. The gentle Parthasarathi used to join them at the camp, where he had obtained a brief fame for saving a life. The story went that he had stood for five whole minutes over a ditch, holding a log in his trunk, refusing to fit the log in the ditch. Only when the forest workers looked in the ditch did they find there a sleeping dog, curled up and snug as a snail.

Now Parthasarathi was getting old, his vision foggy and his legs gone frail, a pink swelling at his temple like the knot on an old kindal tree. So he and the Gravedigger were assigned to work the festivals.

Elephant Sabu's wife was appalled by the Gravedigger's price. Thirty-eight lakhs? For thirty-eight lakhs, they could have bought a parcel of land, as her father had suggested, plus a car. Yet Elephant Sabu believed the tusker's near-perfect physique would in time reap enough profit for multiple cars. After all, the elephant met every single one of the twelve auspicious traits:

1. Prominent bulge between eyes
2. Head held high
3. Large ears that can touch over bridge of trunk
4. Tusk shape: outward and up, whitish color
5. Nice dip on crown of head
6. Eyes honey colored and wide
7. Trunk reaches ground and curls up

8. Over 10 feet high at shoulder
9. Strong thick legs
10. Long body and rounded back
11. Tip of tail like a paintbrush, reaching to ankle
12. Whitish nails, 4 and 4 on front feet, 5 and 5 on

back = 18

    = Auspicious Number

Elephant Sabu was a veritable encyclopedia of pachydermal knowledge. Yet this was wasted on his wife, who didn't even let him get to number 5 before she told him where he could stuff the rest.

§

In a thicket tucked away from the festival mayhem, the Grave-digger ate his panna, becalmed by his bath and the sluggishly munching presence of Parthasarathi. They spent most of their hours in shared company, whether standing still during a puja or sleeping in their adjacent stalls. They bathed together. They drank together. They dozed side by side. When the Gravedigger began to wring his head for dark, cloudy reasons, Parthasarathi rumbled at a frequency only the Gravedigger could perceive. He focused on the hum and the rest of the raucous world fell away.

The Gravedigger found a similar reassurance in the musk of Old Man, who sat on a low wall, his arms around his knees, watching as always.

§

With all sixteen elephants bathed and blessed, the puja began.

The priests took turns feeding the Gravedigger packed balls of rice and brown sugar, laced with turmeric. The last in line, a boy priest, sheepishly raised a hunk of brown sugar to the Gravedigger's mouth. Still chewing, the Gravedigger plucked the hunk and kept it curled in his trunk. Awestruck, the boy priest backed away.

Women broke into riotous birdsong, backed by beating drums. They raised their folded hands, their murmurs overlapping. The Gravedigger felt a pressure inside his head, receding only when the stick paused against his trunk. The stick served as a reminder: *Stand and obey.*

The people wrapped around him, parted wherever he walked, each face resembling the next, like river stones washed smooth of distinction. Someone gave three short shoves to his tusk; he knelt to allow the head priest to mount his front leg as another clambered up his flank, and the frontpiece was unfurled over his forehead in a spill of pink stitching and hot brass, and his legs were locked in baubled anklets, and the heavy gold thidambu was hoisted onto his back. Then he was led to join the fifteen others who awaited him down below, in the dusty expanse that they would have to cross, step by measured step.

· · ·

The drums were deafening, but nothing compared with the barrel rockets so thundersome they skewered the heart, they passed through the body like an explosion, like the explosion that stopped his mother's breath. Smoke threaded up the trees behind the temple. He thought of metal and gunpowder, sun and shadow, all of it throbbing in the skull. How open this sprawl of land, as empty as the uplands where his mother fell. How thick the forest of people, hundreds on the farther side.

One was a little boy, trying to hide behind his mother. She forced him out from her skirts, saying, "Look at the big one, look!" But the boy did not want to look at Sooryamangalam Sreeganeshan. He had seen enough of the beast, who had been haunting the boy's dreams ever since the festival posters had gone up around town. The elephant's tusks seemed to push through the surface of the poster, long and curved like a villain's mustache, with a bubble floating over its clefted head, filled with a threat:

I AM COMING.

The Filmmaker

Fresh from the wedding, Teddy sat at the foot of my bed, where Ravi had been sitting five hours earlier. His left hand was gloved in an elaborate, effeminate henna tattoo. "Sanjay told me all the guys were doing it, like it was a tradition or something. Turns out it's more of a girl thing."

"Why didn't you ask the tattoo lady?"

"I wasn't sure she spoke English." Without his camera, Teddy could be maddeningly shy with the locals. He sniffed his hand and made a face.

"So you had fun," I said.

"I wish I'd been here."

I was disheveled and tired, but no longer wallowing in nausea. I reassured Teddy that the unni appams had long left my system, that Ravi had taken good care of me.

"Ravi," he said, supremely dubious. "Really."

"So did Sanjay come in on a horse?"

"An elephant. He was scared shitless." As Teddy described the scene, my phone buzzed for the third time that morning. I silenced it immediately. Ravi had already messaged me twice, inviting me to go for a drive before Teddy returned. I'd declined, eager to go but worried that the two of us joyriding around Kavanar Park might give rise to suspicion.

"Why aren't you picking up?" Teddy said.

"Oh, it's probably a spammer."

"It's Ravi." Teddy pointed at Ravi's name glowing green on the top of my phone.

I feigned surprise and answered it.

Ravi was curt, all business. "I spoke with the divisional range officer, Samina Hakim. You can make an interview with her. She also suggested that you speak with two of the officers. They can take us on a tour of Kavanar."

"When?"

"Monday. One week from today."

"Okay, great. I'll tell Teddy."

"One more thing: I'm coming over tonight."

"Yup. Got it."

"And he's not invited."

Before I could reply, Ravi hung up.

I relayed most of the conversation to Teddy, who was frowning. "Are you avoiding him or something?"

"Ravi? No, why?"

"He was kind of short with you, from what I could hear."

"Nah." Confronted by Teddy's questioning gaze, I was struck by a phrase from film class—*circles of confusion.* It was poetic for a technical term, meant to determine what zone of a shot would be in focus, or, as the handbook put it, "acceptably sharp." But every lens was imperfect; the image was never perfectly sharp, merely permissible to the eye.

"Stop looking at me like that," I said.

"Like what?"

Rule of thumb, our professor had said. *For close shots, focus on the subject's eyes.*

"Like you're filming me."

He smirked and gave my knee a little shake, resting his henna-gloved hand a little longer than necessary.

On Monday, as promised, Ravi took us to the Range Forest Office, where a flamboyant gulmohar tree stood guard out front. The tree seemed plucked from folklore with its monstrous blossoms, its hunchback trunk, the roots that slithered and splayed down the steps where we stood.

Teddy ran the camera's gaze from the blossoms to the office and back to the blossoms. I cast about for street sounds. Occasionally I glanced at Ravi, who was smoking by the curb, tuned out and gazing mildly ahead. He caught my look and returned a quick, complicit smile.

We'd gotten good at sneaking around. Back at the center, there was a guest cottage, where the walls were woven bamboo, the bed soft, the windows shuttered. It had a quaint, pastoral quality, albeit disrupted by the dotted boxers on the floor and the tongue scraper on the edge of the sink. (I found it weird and endearing that he brought his tongue scraper to our sleepovers. "You don't clean your tongue?" he asked me, prim with shock.) It was cool whenever I stepped inside, the air humming with possibility, a sensation I carried back to my suite before dawn. I never saw Teddy on those nights, which led me to assume, with blissful indifference, that Teddy had never seen me.

Finished with exteriors, we met Ravi at the foot of the steps. "Shall we?" Ravi said, grinding his cigarette underfoot.

Teddy frowned. "Shall we what?"

"Meet with Samina Madame," Ravi said.

"She speaks English, right? So we don't need an interpreter."

Teddy glanced at me. "It's best to have some privacy during these interviews. The smaller the audience, the better."

Ravi grinned like we were being ridiculous. "I know Samina Madame very well. What is so private she couldn't tell me?"

There was an edge to Ravi's voice. He looked to me, as did Teddy, awaiting my call.

"I have your number," I said to Ravi. "You could grab a bite, come back?"

"Grab a bite," Ravi repeated.

"A snack or something—"

"I know what it means," he said, already walking away.

Before Teddy could muse on what had crawled up Ravi's ass, I was climbing the steps.

Inside, an old man in green uniform sat at a desk, behind stalagmites of time cards and file folders. He seemed unperturbed by that wilderness of paperwork or maybe half blind to it, being that his right eye was glazed in white. He fixed us with his stern working eye as we introduced ourselves, then led us down the hall, past a room with an enigmatic sign over the door: WIRELESS. The room was empty, aside from a chair that seated four cell phones in a row, all suckling from a single power strip.

We rounded a corner and entered an office to find Samina Hakim quickly blotting her lipstick on a napkin. She raised her gaze and smiled. There was a dollish prettiness to her features— bow mouth, wide eyes—planted in an ample face. She shook each of our hands, pausing briefly over Teddy's henna before refreshing her smile.

Ms. Hakim said she had only a limited window of time, so we sprang into action. Teddy set up the camera while I softened her up with chitchat, which she seemed happy to make. Among other things, we discussed the magnificence of South Indian coffee. "In America, coffee is not just coffee," she opined. "You ask for coffee, they ask: What size? You ask for milk, they ask: How fatty? Here, coffee is coffee."

"Excellent coffee," I affirmed, clipping a lav mic between the pleats that spread fanlike over her chest. She looked at the fly-sized lav with a degree of suspicion.

"This way I can focus on you," I explained, "instead of holding a mic in your face."

"I see. No problem."

After checking her levels, I asked Ms. Hakim if she'd like to begin. She straightened up, shoulders back, and clasped her hands on the desk like a newscaster, all her warmth displaced by wooden courtesy.

TRANSCRIPT OF INTERVIEW WITH SAMINA HAKIM, DIVISIONAL RANGE OFFICER

SAMINA HAKIM: I am Samina Hakim, Divisional Range Officer for Kavanar region. We work closely with the Wildlife Rescue and Rehabilitation Center, which was established in partnership with the Kerala Forest Department.

Just like that, her personality turned automated as she summarized her father's work as a ranger, her own brief stint as a software engineer in Techno Park, and her quick ascent to becoming the first female range officer in India, at which point she sat back, as if she'd finished her meal and were waiting for the check.

I was caught off guard by her sudden brusqueness and, in fumbling for something to say, happened on a cliché—

EMMA: Your father must be proud.

—which caught Samina off guard. There was a long pause.

SAMINA: My father is not alive. He was killed in a gunfight with poachers in 1992.
EMMA: Oh, I'm so sorry . . . Was that the year you applied?
SAMINA: Yes. (*Pause.*) This is a film about the Rescue Center, no?
EMMA: It is, but we're also interested in the people who come in contact with the center. Of course you're not obligated to discuss anything you don't want to. I just find your background compelling, especially as a woman stepping into unfamiliar territory.
SAMINA HAKIM: The territory suits me very well.
EMMA: Yeah, it looks like poaching has gone way down under your tenure. How've you made that happen?
SAMINA HAKIM: We have increased the number of cases registered, and we have established protection strategies and anti-poaching camps.
EMMA: I've heard people say you're a lot more effective than your predecessor—Mr. P. K. Kurian?
SAMINA HAKIM: I will not comment on that. Simply I have made wildlife and conservation my topmost priority.
EMMA: Did Mr. Kurian have a different priority?
SAMINA HAKIM: No, no, I will not say that. I prefer to focus on positive things, such as, for example, we have been making great strides in protecting forest areas from habitat destruc-

tion. We are involving local communities by training them in sustainable extraction methods of nontimber forest products including honey and cardamom, and, as such, we are making the protection of the forest a priority for all people.

EMMA: I see.

SAMINA HAKIM: Any more questions? I have limited time today.

EMMA: Of course, sure . . .

(*Extended pause.*)

Just switching gears for a second . . . I was reading about a particular case involving the Shankar Timber Company.

SAMINA HAKIM: . . .

EMMA: It was about a protest by a number of villagers who were upset that the Forest Department had allowed a timber company to cut down all the trees on what they perceived—

SAMINA HAKIM: Where did you read this?

EMMA: I don't remember where actually.

SAMINA HAKIM: You know what? These villagers are upset because they see the profit from cutting timber. They want license to do so as well. The Forest Department cannot allow unregulated removal of timber and degradation of the forest. We only give clearance after careful consideration as to whether the outcome is in the public interest.

EMMA: Were the villagers consulted? Or even warned?

SAMINA HAKIM: No.

EMMA: Isn't that a violation of your conservationist principles, like the involvement of local communities—

SAMINA HAKIM: I have answered enough. I think we are finished.

EMMA: There's nothing more you'd like to add?

SAMINA HAKIM: Off it. Off the camera, please.

. . .

As we left the office, Teddy peppered me with questions, all to do with where I'd gotten my intel on Shankar Timber. I told him I'd explain later, when Ravi wasn't waiting by the car.

I hadn't planned to bring up the Shankar Timber case, but as the interview went on, and her answers took on the practiced cadence of a recitation (*as such . . . such as . . . as such*), I'd realized there was no other way of cracking her Teflon veneer. No way but one. The scandal was fair game; it had been in the news, after all. I hadn't jumped her while she was at home in a bathrobe. She had to know the topic might come up.

And yet, judging by her response—the way her hands fused into a gridiron clasp—it was clear she hadn't foreseen this turn at all.

Nor had I considered how my questions might affect Ravi, and his opinion of me. It only made sense to keep him in the dark, for the time being.

An hour later, Ravi, Teddy, and I were strolling through Kavanar Wildlife Park behind Officer Soman and Officer Vasu. Teddy took sound, and I filmed as we filed through the green, all of it undulating just beyond our reach. I'd missed the cool of being behind the camera, hyperattuned to our surroundings and yet detached. There was so much to capture: frothy white bursts of Communist green, so named, Ravi explained, because of its tendency to spread. Macaques rattling the highest branches of the teaks. Nests of silky white orchids sprouting from the branches of trees with roots like lava spills gone solid; red ants threading through a spewage of buffalo dung.

And then there was Officer Vasu and Officer Soman, both of whom had the quaint, bulbous features of garden gnomes. I paid more attention to Officer Vasu, only because he seemed the friendlier of the two. Through Ravi, I asked him about the giant rifle that hung from his shoulder, how often he'd had to use it against poachers. Officer Vasu received each question with a bashful smile and a lift of his nearly hairless eyebrows. "Once or twice," he said. "But not directly at a poacher."

"Why not?"

"If we kill someone, the media gets involved, then the Human Rights Commission. We can lose our jobs. There are many barriers for us."

Without elaborating on the barriers, Officer Vasu walked on. I noted the laces of his shoes were tied haphazardly, woven through random holes and wrapped threefold around the ankles so they wouldn't slip off. What did a poacher have to fear from a guy with oversized camo shoes and putty lumps for brows?

Farther along, Officer Soman pointed out the leaning wreckage of bamboo, thick as elephant bones, thirty years old and weeks away from decay. "Elephants love the bamboo," Ravi added, "so the shortage is drawing them to the farms. And the Forest Department isn't replanting, so—"

What followed was a volley of heated voices, passing so rapid fire we could only film and ask for translation later:

SOMAN: Everyone blames the Forest Department.
RAVI: I'm not blaming—
SOMAN: You know well as I do any decision like that must come from Trivandrum.

RAVI: I just say how I see it. The farmers say the same thing about the bamboo.

SOMAN: Hah! Bunch of IIT geniuses, those people! They also say we should build a Great Wall of China around the park. What is this—a zoo?

VASU: Calm yourself, Soman. They're filming.

SOMAN: They don't care what we say. We won't be in their film.

VASU: Why not?

SOMAN: People like them don't make movies about people like us.

VASU: How would you know? You don't even watch movies.

SOMAN: I know that piece of grass in your mouth doesn't make you Sunil Shetty.

VASU: People can cry and fight all they want, but there will come a time when the bamboo will disappear, then the elephants, then us, and all will be as it was before we arrived. Or maybe it will be something different.

SOMAN: So?

VASU: The world is changing. If it was not changing, it would not be the world.

(*Silence.*)

SOMAN: Someone give this man a Filmfare Award.

After the hike, our hosts took us to rest at their quarters, a two-level bamboo dwelling on stilts. An officer was perched in the lookout tower. We passed by a small garden, displaying neat rows of beans, curry leaves, and cabbages, staked in the center with a strung-up can of Shakti mustard oil, bouncing sunlight as it swung.

Officer Vasu led the tour. Here were the mosquito nets rolled up over the cots; here were the beige shirts hanging from the wall pegs, the bullet shells on the bed, the walkie-talkies spitting sounds, the calendar on the wall with a young girl shyly fondling her braid. And here was the small shrine by the doorway, on a shelf nailed to the wall, with propped pictures of Ganesh and a blue cherubic Krishna, boxes of incense and burnt matches planted in balls of wax. Here they prayed before entering the forest.

As we filmed, it came out that Officer Vasu was from a poor family, same as Officer Soman, who saw his own family once a month. Officer Vasu pulled out a wafer-thin wallet, and from it he extracted what seemed to be a single puzzle piece.

"Me," he said.

And it was him, albeit a younger him, trim and proud in his beige uniform, his foot hitched on the bumper of a jeep. He had cut around his own shape and that of the jeep attached to his foot, as if they were one. I pulled focus on the photo, held delicately in his fingers, dirt under the nails. There was something so humble, so heartwarming, about both Vasus, large and small, now and then, neither of whom seemed capable of harm. Yet two days later, Officer Vasu would shoot a poacher dead. At first I wouldn't believe it; the shooter had to be some other Vasu, not our Vasu, not Vasu of the clown-sized camo shoes. Even in the space of a few hours, I thought I'd come to know him. Had he been playing to the camera? Or had I cast him as the sweet, clumsy native before he'd even opened his mouth?

The jeep trundled us homeward in the late afternoon. The moon made an early cameo, a translucent scoop of vanilla melting into the blue. Ravi had mellowed toward me, and riding beside him, I almost forgot about Teddy in the backseat, wearing that sated look he always got at the end of a good day. Ravi steered with one hand, pointing out the cotton silk trees, the sals, the white pines, and the occasional aanjili, guarded by thuggish monkeys.

We came to idle behind an open lorry, four boys crammed in the back, heels bopping against the bumper. Three of them were chatting; the fourth was distracted by a silky seed floating past. I thought of that Helen Levitt photograph: four girls walking down a street, distracted by passing soap bubbles. Helen Levitt had been twenty-five, around my age, when she bought a Leica. She fit a winkelsucher to her camera, a device that let her point herself in one direction while the photo snapped from the side, so the subject was oblivious to being photographed.

I have almost no photos of our time in India. I told myself I didn't want to be *that* tourist, snapping exotica for the benefit of friends back home, who'd get bored after flipping through a dozen or so. Teddy and I saw our India only in terms of the film, admittedly a narrow lens. We made up for our insecurities by being dogged in purpose: to get everything we could, and get it right.

And yet there were unexpected moments I still wish I could have captured somehow, in a medium more lasting than memory. Like the boy in the lorry, reaching for the silk seed. Or Ravi reaching over the gearshift and squeezing my hand, before Teddy could see.

For dinner, Ravi took us to his favorite restaurant, Y2K, a cryptic name belied by perky flower settings and plastic gingham table-cloths. Our server brought three "home-style meals"—a hillock of rice accessorized with various stews and curries—and diplomatically set spoons beside two of the plates. Ravi ate with nimble fingers that never seemed to still, always tossing or crushing or rounding up a bite, leaving little room for talk.

We were halfway into the meal when Teddy said, "Okay, Em, fess up." My stomach dropped, knowing where he was headed. I'd forgotten to warn him, neglected to explain. Now my signals—beseeching eyes, rigid head shake—were all too late. "Where'd you get that stuff about Shankar Timber?"

Ravi's head snapped up.

Slowly I spooned more pickle onto my plate. "I don't remember."

"You asked her about Shankar Timber?" Ravi said.

Teddy turned to Ravi. "Have you heard about this? There's a village called, what was it—"

"Manaloor," Ravi said.

"Right. Anyway, the discussion got pretty tense, but Emma didn't back down. She's an excellent interviewer, way better than me."

I shook my head at Teddy. "He doesn't wanna hear this."

"What makes her so excellent?" Ravi asked. A brittle note had entered his voice.

"Well, generally speaking, people tend to spill their guts around her."

"Jesus, Teddy, you're making me sound like an operator."

"She's a master of the pregnant pause, for example. People always feel the need to fill a silence, so they end up saying more than they mean to. And there's this other tactic: at the end of an interview, she usually goes, *Is there anything else you think I should know?*"

"It's an honest question," I said.

"It's all in the tone—like, *Hey, you can trust me.* But also, *I know there's something you're not telling me.*"

"So she manipulates people," Ravi said.

Teddy shrugged. "All film is manipulated to some degree. It's a way of cutting closer to the truth."

"Yes, well. Too close and you get a girl cutting her wrists."

Teddy's spoon hung in the air for a moment, before lowering to the table. He looked at me, then Ravi. The silence was a vise, tightening with every second.

"I'm done," Teddy said, tossing his spoon on the plate, and left to wait in the car.

I shook my head at Ravi.

"What?" he demanded.

"I can't believe you."

"I can't believe *you.*"

"I'm sorry . . ."

Ravi rose.

"I didn't tell Samina you told me."

He waved me off and left to rinse his hand at the sink.

I'd been on a string of endless plane trips and car rides, but no voyage had ever felt as long as the thirty minutes it took to get home. I kept glancing at Teddy in the rearview, thinking that if I could just catch his eye, we'd be all right. But Teddy was turned toward the window, his blind gaze fixed on nothing.

The Poacher

We drove Leela to the hospital in Synthetic Achan's car. On the way she began to bleed. She braced her arm against the car door, her face flushed and ugly with pain. My mother gripped her hand. Jayan hugged the wheel.

A hemorrhage, the doctor called it. She had bled out nearly a quarter of her womb's supply. The baby was alive, but there was a high chance that in two weeks' time she would deliver a thing too small to survive. Even if the baby lived, he would be too soft in the head to know his father from a fence post.

They fed tubes into Leela's arms and kept her for the night. In the waiting area I watched Jayan run his thumb along the edge of the car key, up and down and up and down, his face betraying no feeling. At some point he went in to see her alone. He emerged even more sunken than before and said she wanted her underthings and toothbrush.

Leaving Leela with my mother, I drove through the murky dawn. Jayan sat very still in the passenger seat. I was dazed with fatigue, but his murmur roused me instantly.

"I should have killed that elephant. I should have killed him when you came and asked me."

"I was asking you to find someone else—"

"It thinks it can trample my farm and family, end my life as easily as snipping a thread . . ."

"It's an animal. I doubt it has a strategy."

"Then you don't know a thing about elephants."

"But what will Leela say?"

He turned a fierce eye on me. "Who will tell her?"

We passed empty houses painted in the color of cake icings, a church helmed by a huge neon lady sprinkling lights from her fingers. This was the Virgin Mother, whose picture Leela kept in her mirror, a white woman with eyes glassy and mournful for her son.

Our silence lasted until I pulled up to the house. As the engine died, we stared at the scene, same as we had left it, and suddenly it seemed that the whole horrible night had been a dream.

"She thinks the baby is dying inside her," Jayan said.

"She is emotional. Any mother would be."

"Who would know better than her—you? The doctor?" He hung his head, his voice no more than a rasp. "A mother knows these things."

Refusing my comfort or counsel, Jayan scrubbed the wet from his eyes with the heels of his hands and squinted hard at our broken palm. The set of his jaw declared his intentions as did the muscle twitching under his eye. He would inflict an equal pain. He would bleed the creature white.

I asked him if he had an extra green half pant.

He looked at me. "Are you sure?"

My heart was speeding. I was sure of nothing. Yet I could not let him walk alone.

For a wage of five thousand rupees Jayan enlisted Alias, a fellow who knew the forest as if he had designed it himself. As a bonus he came with his own homemade gun. He was famous for his rosewood muzzle-loaders, five feet long, a height nearly reaching his own. He was equally famous for having only eight fingers. It was said that he had lost his last two digits while scrambling up the side of a mountain. Having wedged his hand between two rocks, he pulled and pulled, then pulled out his knife.

Was he Tamil? Tribal? Superhuman? In regard to Alias, my brother advised me to know less.

Synthetic Achan furnished his own gun for Jayan, a piece he said was specially crafted in Germany. He introduced me to the German in the privacy of his rice shed, carrying on about her origins, unaware that the rifle and I had already met. I thought of Raghu aiming the barrel at my enemies—*Take a bet, pussy man.* With sad affection, I traced one of the rabbits that leapcd between the iron leaves.

"Are you listening, boy? Hold out your hand." My uncle dropped a pouch of heavy bullets into my palm. "Use what you need but don't waste. In the sixties, a bullet cost five rupees; now it's seventy. What do you think a gun like this cost?" I nearly spat when he told me: thirty-five thousand. "And that was *back then*."

All throughout this presentation, my uncle kept fiddling with his nose—scratching, twitching, scrunching—so obvious in his anxiety that, in seesaw effect, I was lifted to a state of calm. "One more thing. Tell your brother to bury the bullet deep. Can't let the greenbacks find it. If they find it, I am finished."

I reassured him that all would turn out as planned.

But first I had to get the German past Leela. It was no small task to smuggle the piece from my uncle's Maruti and into our shed. Two days had passed since Leela returned from the hospital, and surely she would have noticed our doings were she not confined to bed rest. There was a pall about her as she waited for the bleeding to start again, for the baby to vanish inside her like a drop of water. Yet her eyes remained sharp and watchful, her wifely sense undiminished.

One evening my mother had me deliver to Leela a bowl of broken-rice soup. As was my habit, I stole a salty spoonful before giving her the bowl. When I turned to go, she caught me at the threshold: "Get me another spoon. You are sick."

In fact, my tonsils had been feeling knobby that morning. "How did you know?"

She raised the bowl and blew across the broken rice. "I know when you are hiding something."

"Hiding?"

"Why else would you be off so quickly?"

"To find you a spoon."

"Don't get smart. Look at me, Manu."

I felt I was standing before a magistrate judge, so stern was her voice.

"What is it?" she said.

"What is what?"

"This thing you are hiding. Is it to do with him?"

"Do I have to say? Mother will hang me."

"What makes you think I won't?"

After some song and dance I conjured up a girl I was planning to meet near the snack stall a half mile from home. Leela viewed me through suspicious eyes. "Do you want to marry her?"

"Maybe."

"Would her parents be happy with you?"

"How should I know?"

"Cut the innocent act. She deserves the truth. Even if she's too stupid to ask for it."

Leela looked down at her bowl and stirred the soup with my infected spoon. After a while she said, "Everyone thinks I trapped your brother. But how can a mouse trap a rat? At least he knew what I was."

"A bricklayer's daughter." I glanced at the door, uneasy. My mother could have stood within earshot.

"Bricklayer." Leela snorted. "My father was no bricklayer. He never lifted a thing aside from his fist."

After our talk, Leela began to suspect my brother of misdoings no matter the time of day. She turned about and about in bed, occasionally shuffling to the doorway on the pretense of seeking fresh air, searching for our return from the fields.

One morning the window presented my mother with a nauseating sight: a Forest Department jeep grumbling up to the front of our house. My mother found she could not move. *What had Jayan done?* His old sins rushed through her in a breathtaking wave.

"Who is it?" Leela called from the bed.

The car door opened, and out came a fat black shoe, mannish if not for the mud-spattered sari hem that fell over it.

"Who?"

"Hush," was all my mother managed to say, for it was the high priestess of the greenbacks aka the lardy little Muslim aka Divisional Range Officer Samina Hakim.

Samina Madame was widely deemed an improvement over her predecessor, a weasel who wore Ray-Bans too fine for his salary and rarely left his roost. Often she was seen stepping into a farmer's house and taking tea on the veranda and listening to the local complaints with her forehead as neatly pleated as her starched olive sari. Why she had arrived at our home was a mystery. My mother decided to parry any and all attacks with an offer of tea, which Samina Madame accepted.

"Sit, sit," said my mother, gesturing to my father's chair.

"Thank you," said Samina Madame, not sitting, "but I came to see how Leela is doing."

Samina Madame smiled winningly, her face a pleasant pie. For a heavyset woman there seemed not an ounce of extra to her.

My mother showed Samina Madame into Leela's room and made a hasty introduction. Leela sat up straight. It was a tremendous blow to receive her enemy while prone and clad in a nightgown.

"Let me get the tea and biscuits," my mother said and fled.

"Do I look like I need more biscuits?" called Samina Madame jovially.

She dragged a plastic chair next to Leela's bed and sat. Here, Leela felt, was the harpy responsible for the imprisonment of her husband. The one who had snuffed him out through her sneaks and snitches, had handed him to the Karnataka police like a neat kilo of cake.

"I went to the hospital," Samina Madame said. "They said you were here. How are you?"

"Fine. Alive. Most people who see the Gravedigger cannot say the same."

"What luck your husband woke up when he did."

Though it was I who had awoken first, Leela nodded.

"And," Samina Madame said, "the baby?"

Leela stared straight through Samina Madame, who leaned back, made aware that she had crossed into forbidden waters.

Both women turned quiet. Samina Madame's gaze casually traveled the walls. Leela ran a hand over her bedsheet, a new cool cotton scattered with sailboats. She knew the rule: Never buy gifts for an unborn baby. But she had seen these sailboats and disobeyed.

"Is your husband home?" Samina Madame asked.

"In the fields."

"Will he come back for lunch?"

"You plan to stay till lunch?"

"I don't have to." Samina Madame smiled uncomfortably and rocked a little in her seat like a hen ridding itself of an egg.

"He works through lunch."

"And how has your husband been doing since he came home?"

"You should know that, madame." Leela uttered *madame* as if it were the dictionary definition of manure. "He came by your office two weeks after his release. Yours is the office with the gulmohar tree?"

Madame nodded, her brightness turning uncertain. "I don't remember him coming."

"He was looking for a job with the Forest Department. No one knows the inner regions like him, so he thought he might be a watcher, help patrol in the forest. Isn't that one of the jobs you people offer?"

"Yes, as part of a pilot project aimed to harmonize the economic needs of local people with the needs of wildlife—"

"Your peons laughed in his face."

"Who laughed? Which guard?"

"What difference would it make? All are the same."

"Oh, I think it obvious I am not."

"Because you take tea with us and ask about our health? I hear you also take tea with those Shankar Timber people."

Madame faltered, plainly surprised on several fronts—that this invalid was interrogating her, that the invalid was on a first-name basis with the scandal that had attached itself to Madame's heel like so much dog shit. "That was beyond my control."

"I hear you take more than tea from them, madame."

"The working plan is approved at multiple levels—Delhi, Trivandrum. I was against the felling, but I was overruled. Of course it is easy for you to sit and make accusations. Much harder to come up with solutions."

"I come up with them all the time."

"Then tell me."

"We need electric fences around the farmlands and roads," Leela said. Madame nodded. "Not the cheap stuff, the kind a baby boar could eat through." Madame's nodding was hypnotic. Leela found herself talking against her will. "And another thing: you should give people like my husband some opportunity. He would be of use. People like him—they want to lead a right life, they want to listen to your advices, but advices don't fill the belly. You have to give them some way to live right."

"And you are sure he wants to live right?"

"What kind of question is that?"

"No need to get hot."

But Leela was sick with self-loathing. She had succumbed to this smarmy woman, this sari-clad greenback with tricks up her sweater sleeve.

"It's fact. Majority of poachers are repeat offenders. They make the same mistakes again and again whether they want to live right or not."

"He paid his dues."

"Trust me, he still has his debtors, his enemies. They keep an eye on him."

"And you keep them in your pocket."

"I keep them close," Madame said. "Some of them anyway. They are like chin hairs, these people. Pluck one, and four more pop up in its place."

"Why have you come, madame? To talk about chin hairs?"

"To see what you know about your husband." Madame frowned. "Very little, it seems."

"I know he fell in with some bad people. They took advantage just because he was good at shooting birds and monkeys, an elephant here and there—"

"Fifty-six."

Leela sat back, blinking. The number stole her breath. "Four," she insisted weakly. "Five maybe."

"His associate told the judge fifty-six. And lately your husband has been meeting with a man who has killed even more. Now what do you think they're discussing?"

"I . . . I don't know."

As my mother's footsteps approached, Madame laid her business card on the side table, signaling the end of the topic. "Not the weather, I can assure you."

The Elephant

Old Man had only himself to blame for the hiring of Kizhak-kambalam "Romeo" Kuriakose. Romeo had a straight white smile, which Old Man had mistaken as a sign of good hygiene when in fact it was a set of false teeth. Bone disease had taken all his teeth at age twenty, Romeo claimed, a blessing in disguise as now he had the smile of a prince!

The princely smile faded as soon as Old Man put a shovel in his hands and told him to tow the Gravedigger's poo.

An elephant won't stand for waste in its midst, said Old Man. In the forest they never foul the same place twice. Proper as Brahmins.

Romeo turned the shovel upside down and frowned at the metal end. What does that make us?

Elephant Sabu required three pappans per elephant. For the third pappan, Old Man wanted a younger lad, someone malleable and curious about the work. Before Old Man had even begun his search, Romeo dragged in the dregs of his family: his brother and his brother's son, a baggy-eyed boy who had failed eighth standard for three straight years and kept his eyes on his feet. The boy had the shape of an urn, burly and broad shouldered, bereft of a neck. For all his apparent strength, he flinched like a chicken in his father's presence. His father called him a dolt, said the boy never listened to his parents no matter how they striped his backside. Wouldn't Old Man please take the dolt under wing and tame him the way he'd tamed so many uncivilized beasts?

Your name? Old Man asked the boy.

Mathai.

Do you have an interest in elephants?

Don't know. Never met one.

His father smacked the back of his head. What kind of answer is that? (A reasonable one, Old Man felt.)

Mathai, said Old Man, weighing the name. We will call you Mani.

A Hindu name? the boy asked. You trying to convert me?

No, idiot, said Romeo, though he'd asked the same question on his own first day. It's so when we take the elephant to temple, those swamis won't think you a swine-eating Nasrani.

Mani-Mathai cracked a shy smile. Only Catholics eat swine.

. . .

So the poo towing and food gathering fell to Mani-Mathai, who took the job and sponged up whatever knowledge Old Man had to offer: that an elephant always rinses its own feet before drinking water, proper as a Brahmin; that an elephant can hold ten liters of water in its trunk; that one should never bend to pick up anything that falls at an elephant's feet, lest one's head be used as a step stool.

Old Man was pleased with Mani-Mathai, who more than made up for the toothless drunk that was his uncle. Romeo bought the loyalty of other pappans through a steady supply of dirty jokes and bidis, an argot of girlie magazines. When not slinging abuse at his nephew, he ignored the boy, who kept to himself.

Over time, Old Man began to realize that Mani-Mathai was no dolt. His father mistook his quiet for stupidity, his mindfulness for laziness. Whereas most boys his age were as fidgety as leaves in a breeze, Mani-Mathai had a steadiness about him. For hours, he could sit with the elephants, neither bored nor drowsy, simply watching them eat.

Behind his reticence, the boy harbored strange ideas. He once described to Old Man a sound he felt, when in the company of Parthasarathi and the Gravedigger. A kind of throbbing in the air, a shifting hum he could feel in his marrow. "Not all the time," Mani-Mathai qualified, risking a glance at Old Man. "Only sometimes."

Old Man had never felt such a thing, but he wondered.

. . .

As soon as Romeo caught wind of Mani-Mathai's "throbbing," he suggested that the sensation was likely located in the boy's chaddi pant. The other pappans joined in the ridicule. "Feel this?" said Romeo and pitched a rock at his nephew's crotch.

Early the next morning, Mani-Mathai ran away. Early the same evening, his father restored him to Old Man's door, clamped by the nape. There was a plum-colored bulge at the boy's temple.

The days went rainless. Teak leaves scrolled up and fell, hard as turtle shells, dragging themselves over dry earth.

At last a storm pounded through the drought, ransacking the trees of old leaves. Rain clattered against the roof of the pappan shed. A window shutter slammed the sill, waking Old Man, who pulled the shutters closed and slid the rusty hook into place. Romeo lay asleep on his belly, facedown, arms spread in a pose of drowning. As useful in sleep as he was at work.

Mani-Mathai usually slept on a pallet between their beds, but that night, the pallet lay empty. Another escape, no doubt, which would result in another beating. Old Man heaved himself up, sure it was too late, that the boy was just another shadow between the trees by now.

He found Mani-Mathai on the front step, arms around his big knees, staring into the dark. Old Man spoke the boy's true name, Mathai, but the boy turned his face away. Were those tears on his cheeks, or rain?

. . .

Come inside, Old Man said loudly, to be heard over the weather.

Coming, said the boy, without moving.

Old Man imagined himself in bed, sliding down a swift tunnel toward the few hours of sleep that remained. Instead he settled onto the step beside Mani-Mathai and watched the rain thin to needles.

I do hear them, said the boy. I feel the elephants talking.

I believe you, said Old Man.

The boy sucked his teeth. Old people don't believe in anything. They think they know everything.

Who said I am old?

The boy glanced at Old Man and wiped a thick finger under his nose. You look old.

Old Man didn't know how to respond. What would comfort the boy? A hand on the shoulder? A hand on the head? Old Man was still debating shoulder versus head when Mani-Mathai said, Could I have a day off?

Yes. One.

My father says I only get a day off when you do.

. . .

I get a day off when the elephant does.

The boy sighed into the night, his face a study. Was he born in chains?

He was taken as a calf. His mother was shot by poachers. When the forest guards found him, he was by her side.

Do you think he remembers her?

He remembers everything. That is the elephant's great gift.

After a pause in which it seemed the boy's mind had drifted elsewhere, Mani-Mathai said, Terrible gift.

Old Man was taken with the simple truth of those words, laid side by side. For someone so young, so simple, the boy had depths.

The elephant takes to you, said Old Man.

I feel that too.

Old Man let pass a few moments of silence, then said: Did I ever tell you about the time the elephant saved my life?

The boy looked over, wary, and shook his head.

Once we were at a temple, and people were coming up closer and closer to touch his tusk and feed him bananas and get a blessing. I could see he was nervous, the way he stuck his trunk tip in his mouth. I tried to push the people back. I spread my arms, but they pressed in, shouting at me to get out of the way. Next thing I know I am rising through the air. The elephant had plucked me up by the waist and planted me on his back.

What did the people say?

Nothing at all! Like a school of gaping smelt down below. Like a god in flesh had landed among them and me on his back with my rump in the air.

Mani-Mathai gazed off in the direction of the elephant stalls, where eight beasts slept on their sides, eight awesome pumping hearts the size of jackfruits. Do you believe he is a god? the boy asked.

Old Man stopped short of the truth, that there were times when he feared the elephant more than he feared anyone's god. That he sensed something cloudy behind those honey-clear eyes. That, as he was being whisked through the air, coiled up in the trunk, Old Man had thought his moment had come, that the elephant had turned on him: every pappan's deepest fear. What he also felt in that airborne second was the prickling sensation of epiphany: *So this is what he felt for me all along.*

Come, said Old Man. Still a few hours of sleep left.

. . .

Not yet. Mani-Mathai looked at him pleadingly. Tell another story. A long one.

Old Man remembered a similar hunger for stories, his father's low voice wrapping around him like a shawl, restoring magic to the drudgery of their days. Even if no one valued the insights of a pappan anymore, the stories told of a time when they had. To pass these stories along was to hope for better. And Old Man had no son, only this boy with hope-starved eyes.

So Old Man told the story his father had told him so many times, with so many different endings, it seemed to knit itself anew each time he spoke it aloud.

§

Long ago, in the time before tusks, every bull elephant had wings. Taloned, scaly, latticed with veins, they carried the males through the air while the cow elephants watched from below, with casual interest. Such feats they performed in mating times, such aerials and dives!

Until the Sage ruined everything.

The Sage resided in the dark heart of the woods, a puckered pious grump who kept mostly to his own. One day while the Sage was praying, a flying calf dropped a foul load on his head. Some said the calf was a prankster; others said he merely had bad aim (or excellent aim, depending on your opinion of the Sage).

Set on having the last word, the Sage cursed all elephants to a flightless life.

In a matter of days, every elephant wing withered and shrank to a tissuey translucence and molted away. Elephants leaped and fell. Their thuds, their shrieks of anguish, silenced even the chattiest of birds for miles.

One of the elephants—we shall call him the Elephant—attempted to negotiate with the Sage. As usual, the Sage was in a temper, but he heard the Elephant out.

The tiger has its stripes, the Elephant complained. The peacock has its tail. The gaur is so ugly you can't tell his rump from his face, but at least he has horns.

What do you want from me? said the Sage.

The wings, O Holy Sage. The wings were our best thing.

Don't O Holy me. Even if I wanted to reverse the curse, which I do not, I cannot. What's cursed is cursed.

Can't you give us something else then? Something beautiful and mighty of our own?

After much flattery and blather, the Sage relented. He poured a fistful of dirt into a cloth pouch. Rub a pinch onto your upper teeth, he said, and see.

. . .

The Elephant did as he was told, and by next morning, two of his teeth had grown into swooping, sparkling tusks of ivory. At first, he was unimpressed. They were beautiful but useless, unlike the broad armor of wings. But that very day, the other forest animals herded around the elephant and marveled at his new equipment. The monkeys hung from them, and the birds perched near the tips. From the depths of the forest, the tigers mewled with envy.

The cow elephants found the tusks quite handsome. The other bulls, noticing this, powdered their own teeth with the Sage's dust, and soon almost every forest bull had tusks of his own— with mixed results. Some yellowy and splayed, some slender and sharp, some blunt, some long, and one poor deformed bastard who starved to death because his tusks crisscrossed directly over his mouth. Everyone agreed that the most imperious of tusks belonged to the Elephant.

Rumor of the tusks reached the Rajah, who invited the Elephant to the palace in order to see these twin miracles for himself. In preparation, the palace floors were polished to a high sheen, the front steps demolished and rebuilt wide enough to fit an elephant's foot. Up the steps the Elephant went, the crowds of commoners cheering down below. Inside the palace, the nobles went up in flaming fits of admiration. One lady fainted; the others stepped over her to marvel at the Elephant. Even the Rajah teared up at the sight. Such a mighty creature, and those tusks, those amazing, impossible tusks!

. . .

They fed the Elephant pomegranate and silky custard and honeyed milk, anything he requested. The Elephant had a grand time, and drowsy with sugar and pleasure, he accepted the Rajah's offer to stay overnight in the temple, which was the only structure with ceilings high enough to contain him.

The next morning, when the Rajah came by, the Elephant began to say his farewells. But the Rajah begged him to stay one more night, as a neighboring prince had heard of the tusks and was just now on his way to the temple. The Elephant consented, for who could say no to the Rajah? Day after day, the Rajah came with another request, and as visitor after visitor passed through the temple, the Elephant began to worry. One night, he tested the temple gates and found them locked. The next morning, he woke to find his ankle chained.

And so, over the years, hundreds of people came to lay fruit at the feet of the Rajah's elephant. They honored him in song and sculpture and painting. Children demanded toy elephants with finger-length tusks, and like the children, every rajah wanted a tusker of his own. They sent hunters into the forests, who dug deep pits, then covered them with branches and baited fruit.

In time, no respectable royal menagerie was without a half-dozen tuskers. The temples followed suit. But none was as beloved as the very first tusker, whom the Rajah cast in a silver coin, so that he might be honored to the end of days.

§

The forest elephants decided that the Sage would have to pay. Chief among them was the All-Mother, who searched the darkest leafy depths until she found the cave in which he had been hiding, too narrow for anything wider than a panther to enter.

One evening, as he tiptoed out, she swatted him to the ground and pinned him beneath the plinth of her foot. The Sage wriggled and screamed. Keep it up, she said, and I'll stamp another hole in your head.

The Sage took shallow breaths.

He was my son, the All-Mother said. He died in that palace, inside their cage. They burned his body in their heathen way. Even his bones! How am I to grieve for my dear one without his bones?

How, the Sage said, unable to continue until the All-Mother removed her foot from his chest. How did you know of the burning?

I smelled his ashes on the wind.

The Sage plopped onto a stone, head in his hands. He hadn't meant for the pits and the arrows and the chains. It was much worse than when he'd grounded the elephants, who did not speak to him for a full ten years afterward. Now the Sage was a fugitive in his own forest.

· · ·

The All-Mother demanded that the Sage rid the tuskers of their tusks, but in these matters, the Sage was powerless. Just as the All-Mother raised her trunk to strike him dead, the Sage cried out, Wait! I have one thing to offer!

Folded between two hills was a lake, unknown to man or animal. The Sage would show her the way, and she would show the way to her kin. In this manner, the elephants would know where to go when death was upon them. Here would be their last resting place, at the edge of the secret lake, where they could sip the blue water and die in peace. Here they could come to grieve undisturbed, and their bones and the bones of their descendants would be safe from human hands.

Said the All-Mother, I don't give a hog's bottom about your death resort! Man will find it, and all he will see is a field of white gold for the taking. He will carve beads and bend bangles from our remains.

The Sage closed his eyes and saw that this was a narrow possibility. Someone would come, but thinking it best not to go into details, he said instead, This is one place most men will not find, but *if* any man should come and thieve even the smallest shard, he will lay it back down, along with his life.

And so it was that the elephant graveyard came to be. In time, all the elephants knew the way to the dead. Some elephants were known to limp for miles, haunches bristling with arrows, trickling blood across farm and forest and scrub grass to reach the secret lake. Just as the Sage had promised, one sip and an elephant could expire in peace.

The location of the graveyard was a secret they guarded so carefully no elephant would speak the directions aloud; it was whispered through the pads of their feet. The elephants became so accustomed to keeping silence that they evolved toward a new language, at a frequency and range no human could hear.

Only one elephant broke the oath, a cow born with a single, dirty yellow tusk of which she was very proud. She had been scrapping with a langur, who refused to believe such a graveyard even existed. She told the langur of the location, but before the langur could swing away and tell its cohorts, the All-Mother sprang from the bush and struck the monkey dead. The loose-lipped elephant begged forgiveness from the herd, but there was no greater sin than spoiling the secret. To seal her silence, they ran her off a cliff.

§

One age passed into the next. Landmasses parted and clashed; mountains rose at the seams. Kings fought and married and begat more kings, their exploits embellished and put to song. But the fatherless boy who concerns us now was no royal, so insignificant he did not even warrant a name.

The boy was in need of work. He had heard of a road being dug and paved many miles from his village, so he set out by foot and any lorry that would have him. Along the way, he met an old woman, slouching down the road in rags. He asked her for directions to the roadwork, and when she raised her face and smiled with a single dirty yellow fang, he wished he had waited for another person to ask. She opened her hand and drew him directions along the tangled seams of her palm lines, to a place she claimed would bring him greater riches than any old road. With no one else to guide him, he took her advice, walking and walking, unable to mark time. The sun seemed fixed in place, a white button sewn on blue sky.

At last, the boy arrived at a lake that none of his people had seen, that he had only known from the stories.

What would he tell them of the elephant graveyard? The silence was of another world. There was a lake so still it seemed of glass, and all around its banks, as far as he could see, giant elephant skulls, eye sockets wide as his head, jaws upon jaws of blunt teeth, long, clean bones, rib cages like caves, and tusks of such phosphorescence they seemed to glow from within.

The boy lifted a piece of ivory no longer than his forearm, a kilo at best. How much money could it bring? Surely more than enough to see his family through the year, at which point he would be old enough to ask the foreman for his father's job.

He ignored the squeeze of terror in his chest. He wrapped the piece in his shirt, tucked it under his arm, and hitched his way back home. The journey lasted several days; he slept at any teahouse that would offer him shelter and sometimes under the stars.

At home, his stepmother unraveled the fabric from the tusk as carefully as if she were removing a bandage from a wound. Her lips parted; she sent out a soft sigh. She clasped the boy's hand, and it seemed to him, against all his prior assumptions, that she did love him after all, that she would never leave as she had so often threatened to do if he did not bring home a proper wage. Now she took to calling him *clever boy* and *my son*, as opposed to the usual *son-of-another-mother* and *orphan boy*.

The next morning, the boy moved through the world with fresh hope, glancing on occasion at the base of their cashew tree, where he had buried the pale marvel by twilight. He considered it their buried potential, a seed that would split and spread with plenty. His stepmother planned to ask her brother about where to sell the ivory, but she warned the boy to keep his sweet mouth shut, so as not to attract unfriendly elements.

Enchanted with her silvery future, the stepmother barely heard the boy complain of an aching head. Early in the evening, the boy took to his bed. He touched his temple to find there a thin channel of fluid, stickier than sweat.

Over the next few days, other changes began to assert themselves. He could not draw a breath without tasting all its flavors, as if the air were rendered clear and specific, as if he could peel away its layers, as if he had lived his whole life with cotton up his nose and now, only now, were his nostrils flushed out. His step-mother was onion and sweat, tempered with fennel. His mother, he remembered, carried a glaze of burnt brown sugar.

And he began to receive flashes of memory, snapshots from a time of life so early no one would believe the memories were his. He remembered the first bewildering time he hiccuped in his mother's womb. He remembered the watery glug of his mother's heart, a slow bass to his frantic ticking, and the metallic scent that met him when he emerged into the world. He remembered her face, haggard and doting, with eyes the shifting hue of a stormy sky.

He shared these developments with his stepmother, who had little use for his tales. Quit stalling, she said, and take the ivory piece to my brother.

But the boy was frightened by his body and mind, how they seemed to be writhing outside their natural, known borders. The next morning, he dug up the tusk and tucked it under his arm. Across forest and field he walked in pursuit of the elephant grave-yard. But the yellow-toothed witch had vanished, along with her directions, and he found himself wandering in circles.

Upon returning home, the boy buried the marvel in a place unknown to his stepmother, who retaliated by withholding his supper and calling him son-of-a-whoremonger. The boy had other concerns. There was his skin, which began to thicken and toughen in places, forming dark, leathery patches across his back, his legs, his forehead. There were his fingernails, growing into hard, yellowish tiles. And every night, there was the ache that pulsed from the roots of his top two canines. They felt strange to the tip of his tongue, a pair of ungainly impostors. In the mirror, they looked whiter than the rest.

Was he boy or elephant? he wondered. Could he be both things at once?

Don't be silly, said his stepmother. No one can be two things at once. For now you are a boy, more or less. But obviously you are turning into an elephant.

This is because of that tusk, the boy said, his eyes watering. It was the tusk that did the damage. What if I return it? Can't I reverse the curse?

Oh, my sweet stupid son, there is no reversing a curse, everyone knows that. But who says we cannot turn this curse into a blessing?

Gently at first, she urged him to try to remember the location of the elephant graveyard. She suggested that he return there, with a wheelbarrow in tow, and take what else he could. You will do the taking, the stepmother said, being that you are already cursed and also my back has been paining me lately, so I will stay home. Think of it, sugar lump! One trip and your poor stepmother would never have to work again. No more work for you either, only a lifetime of mangoes and bananas and rest, free to come and go as you please.

·   ·   ·

That night, the boy lay awake, sifting through his memories for the location of the elephant graveyard, not to fulfill his stepmother's request but to return what he had thieved. He refused to believe his stepmother's claims about curses. He was the hero of his story; he swore to decide his destiny, his end, no matter what happened to his body.

To this oath, his body answered full force.

Before the boy could cry out from the pain, his two long teeth dove and rose into tusks of molten white, so white they glowed in the dark. His spine buckled and rounded; his nose dropped heavy and thick, so much power pent up in each accordion fold. His toes merged, his soles grew soft and sensitive. There was a pleasant kind of twitching at his tailbone. He sneezed.

He rose, instantly falling onto all fours, and shouldered a hole in the roof. With two strikes of his head against the mud wall, he saw his way out into the yard, to the mulberry bush. He learned quickly how to wield his trunk, how to toss away the dirt, how to pinch an occasional berry for his own brief pleasure. At last he found the marvel, glowing against the velvet dirt. Just as he shook it clean, he smelled her on a breeze. Onion and sweat, tempered with gunmetal.

He turned to face his stepmother. She was aiming his father's rifle at him. Her eyes were round and easy to read as they traveled over his tusks, her fear and revulsion sliced with greed.

·   ·   ·

Take me to the graveyard, she said.

There are wants that change from month to month, and then there are yearnings so permanent their power and shape remain hidden from us save for a rare but terrible moment. How much time he had wasted in pursuit of a mother's love, how much effort given to the woman on the other end of that gun. Sorrow overcame him, sorrow and failure and fury, and he roared from every corner of his chest. He took a few charging steps toward his stepmother, and she did as he expected her to do—she fired into his chest.

With the pain came another flash of memory, a recollection that seemed both his and not his, to which his feet responded by thundering into the depths of the wood.

All night he wandered, feeling the life leak out from his chest, feeling his boy memories melt away from him, replaced by others. There were flying elephants, spinning and cresting against blue skies; there was the Sage and the pinch of fateful powder; there was the Rajah, the custard, the cage. All the while, his legs moved of some long-buried volition. A waterbird rode his back, though he saw no water in the vicinity. When his steps began to drag, the bird flew ahead, lone and white against the gold-stained dawn.

Hours passed, or maybe minutes; the elephant could not be sure. All he knew for certain was the smell, which greeted him before the graveyard did—the ghosts of older elephants. His eyes had weakened, but he could just make out the blue haze of lake and sky, the hard white ruins. He sipped from the water and went to lay himself down in the shade cast by the largest skull.

From the hollows of the skull came the All-Mother's smell, ancient and mineral, swelling his lungs. The smell brought other memories: the seams in her trunk, the column of her leg, the leg he used to lean against. He could no longer tell if the light were fading from behind his eyes or from the sky beyond, but all that seemed unimportant now. He circled round a single thought: So *this* was what it was all about! Of course he had to end precisely here, surrounded by her smell and by white on all sides, white as the inside of an egg, as the beginning of another life.

The Filmmaker

On Tuesday, the day after dinner at Y2K, Ravi was called to the eastern side of the park for keeper training, leaving ample time for an argument with Teddy.

"When did you tell him about Shelly?" Teddy demanded.

We were walking back to our rooms after a lukewarm shoot of a keeper bottle-feeding a tiger cub. All morning, I'd been formulating an apology. As soon as I began, he cut me off. "When?"

"When I got sick, I guess, I don't know. We spent a whole day together." Teddy lengthened his stride, making it hard to keep up. "I shouldn't have, I'm sorry."

I followed him into his suite. Whatever room Teddy inhabited, he managed to suffuse it with an air of artistic struggle—the open Moleskine like a flattened bird on his desk, the cryptic note cards across his bed (example: VULTURE SEQUENCE—THEY HATE BEING CAGED), the Batara matchbox on the sill, next to the incense holder/toilet-paper tube that could have, at any given moment, fragrantly burned down the room. Within that chaos of strewn clothes and notes was one corner of order: the suitcase of mini-DV tapes, each of which he had cataloged and kept with persnickety care.

Teddy shoved some note cards aside and sat on his bed, detaching the lens. "Did Ravi tell you about that Shankar Timber stuff?"

I nodded. "I don't think I was supposed to tell you."

"So you two are buddy-buddy now, huh?"

"I guess, yeah." I paused. "He's comfortable with me."

"For obvious reasons."

"Because we're friends."

"I'm your friend. You never used to wear lip stuff around me."

I was surprised, and dismayed, that he'd taken note of my tinted lip balm. "You're being ridiculous. This is how it always happens—they get attached, we get attached." *Don't get too close to the animals,* Ravi had told me, taking gentle hold of my elbow while I stood by the elephant nursery. *We don't want them getting attached.* "How's he supposed to open up if he doesn't trust us?"

"All I'm saying is be careful. You have a way of encouraging people. Whether you mean to or not."

My cheeks went warm. I sensed that Teddy was verging on some sort of confession, something that would capsize our friendship entirely. Clichés ran like ticker tape through my head—*need to be on my own . . . just don't see you that way . . .*

Teddy let out a sigh. "My dad's cutting me off in two months."

"From what?"

"He's been sort of spotting me some cash here and there, when times were tough. But now he has Bev and her whole litter, so pretty soon, that's it. No more loans. No more health insurance."

I sat beside him. "So you'll freelance. You'll move to Greenpoint. You'll eat at McDonald's every Wednesday." I'd been the one to inform him of Fifty-Cent Wednesday, when, for three dollars, you could buy a week's worth of flaccid burgers. "You'll get by like everyone else, until you can't. And then you'll tutor rich kids or whatever."

He nodded, a sad little smirk on his face. "It's just, I'll never have time like this again. Uninterrupted. Financed. At least not anytime soon."

"So?"

"So I need this film to count. This is our chance to make a name for ourselves. A film by Emma Lewis and Teddy Welsh."

"Nice. I get top billing."

He gave me a quick wincing look. "You're taking this seriously, right?"

I was startled by his sincerity and offended and guilty, all of which added up to an exasperated, *"Yes."*

"Sorry. I just had to say it."

Technically I hadn't lied, merely tiptoed around the truth, given him the literal outline rather than the messy essentials. And yet. That doomful sort of feeling. The sudden, itchy need to seek refuge elsewhere, anywhere. I told Teddy I wanted to shoot some B-roll, and before he could mount any serious objection, I whisked the camera away.

On my way to the calves, I stopped by a keeper bent over a steel tub and filmed him hand-sifting rice and mung beans. The brown and the white filled the frame in granulated waves, sliding and mixing, mesmerizing.

I looked up to meet the skeptical gaze of the keeper, whose duck mullet deserved equal skepticism.

"Ana kutty," the keeper said, nodding over his shoulder, in the direction of the elephant calves. He mimed feeding himself from the pail, as in *Feeding time,* or *Don't you have anything better to chronicle for posterity?*

I knew the way to the calves, which turns to take, a sharp left at the bale of new-cut grass, wire fences trailing ahead on either side. But once I reached the calves, I lost the will to film. Instead I rested the camera on a fence post and watched them, for the first time, without any equipment attached to my ears or eyes.

Two keepers held spouted jugs of milk. The younger ones went first, trunks lofted, mouths around the spouts. Milk dribbled onto the wiry hairs of their chins, giving them goatee beards. The bigger calves gurgled mutinous cries, draped their trunks on the drinkers' backs, begging for a turn. The keepers pushed their trunks away while the lucky ones sucked and sloshed.

We'd filmed the feeding before, but I felt the shots could've been tighter, framing out the keepers, focusing on eyes and tongues and trunks, heightening the sounds of snuffle and whimper, as if to enter their circle instead of observing it. I envisioned a film that included patient, lyrical sequences like these, the absence of human voices opening a channel for a more intimate, visual language.

As the calves fed, my phone vibrated against my hip. R VARMA. Just the sight of his green-glowing name erased the bitterness of yesterday's spat. All I felt was a dangerous elation.

I turned my back on the glaring keepers, jogging away from the calves before answering: "Hey, where are you?"

"Driving," Ravi said, a smoky rasp to his voice.

I waited for more, presuming he was calling to make amends. Maybe the fine art of reconciliation was not his forte. "I should've checked with you before mentioning the timber case. I'm sorry."

He grunted.

I entered the empty main office, set the camera on his desk, collapsed into his chair. I would not be the one to speak next. I swiveled and studied the back shelves, which seemed a pencil's weight from buckling, loaded with dusty ledgers, binders, logbooks, old keyboards choked in cords. "About Shelly." No reply. I soldiered on through the silence. "Please don't bring that up again. It's been awkward all day between Teddy and me, and maybe he knows about me and you, or at least has an inkling . . ."

If the conversation were a seesaw, I was stranded at the high end, legs dangling, ridiculous.

"Never mind," I said. "Let's talk tonight."

"I will be home in the morning only."

"Why, what's going on over there?"

"Nothing. The training." His voice trailed off; I could hear him breathing. Ravi wasn't one for meditative pauses, at least not over the phone.

"I received a call," he said finally. "There was a tusker found dead on a farm, in Sitamala."

"The same elephant who killed the kid?"

"No idea. I will do the postmortem in the morning. You can come, if you want."

"Was the elephant killed, or did it die naturally?"

"Killed."

The elephant took shape in my mind's eye, heaped and riddled with holes. I didn't know what to say.

"Tomorrow will be messy," Ravi said. "Wear your ugly shoes."

He hung up before I could ask which of my shoes he considered ugly. I scanned the wall behind the desk, where a goatish creature stared dolefully from the collage of newspaper clippings. The headlines held me captive: "Wild Buffalo Rehabilitates in Dibru Saikhowa." "Displaced Rhino Calf Reunited with Mother." "Man Spears, Man Saves." "First Elephant Calves Released."

Beneath the last headline, this highlighted paragraph:

Four adolescent elephant calves were released to the wildlife park yesterday, wearing radio collars and ear tags. Used to track the vulnerable calves, the radio collars will fall away after several weeks. "The tags will stay for years," says Ravi Varma, head veterinary doctor at the WRRC, "so we can collect long-term data as the calves age and mate and eventually produce calves of their own."

The quote sounded like the sorts of answers Ravi used to give me in the beginning, sanded clean of all personality. I tried to stray from the bases he usually hit during interviews, avoiding a prewritten checklist of questions, but sometimes a question would strike me later, the one I'd neglected to ask. Such a one occurred to me now, what I should've asked him over the phone, what would likely gnaw him all night—was the dead elephant wearing a tag? Was it one of his own?

The Poacher

On Tuesday, the day before we embarked on our hunt for the Gravedigger, an elephant was found dying on Old Raman's farm. It had likely stumbled out of the forest and folded at the edge of the field, felled by its numerous wounds. The shooter had shown little mercy or skill, for the beast died slow, bombarded to the end by so many squinting human eyes.

The greenbacks would suspect Old Raman as accessory in the elephant's death, lumping him with those farmers who had baited bothersome elephants in the past. One had even lodged a firecracker in a jackfruit, thus making a crater of his enemy's mouth. But Raman was cut of a softer cloth. He brought water in a plastic bucket, and when the elephant was too weak to lift its trunk, he crept forward and every so often scooped water over the foamy slab of its tongue.

When first I heard of the dying beast, I hoped it was the Gravedigger. Jayan wanted the opposite; the hunt was all he ever thought about, even when he took me out with his friends. He spent the evening sitting over his glass with shoulders rounded, nostrils aflare, eyes so dark and intent I could see him rehearsing the kill in his head.

Yet his friends made up for his sullenness. We drank and smoked, and they dubbed me Wee Shivaram after I choked on a peg of fuel-flavored booze. I decided to accept the name even if it was lightly demeaning. To be demeaned by those fellows was to be taken under wing, and the more I laughed along, the more it seemed these boys could in time be my boys, Jayan among them. On the way home I fell, twisting my ankle, and had to limp against my brother. We flung our way forward while Jayan howled rubbish at the dark: *Here he comes—the Undertaker, we'll make of him a vulture's dinner!*

But the vultures were already dining by morning. The greenbacks burned sandalwood and ramacham to cover the dead elephant's rot; still it stewed and spread in the heat.

Leela went on foot to see the elephant. She had not spoken one word to us since dawn, when we returned with liquor on our breath and guilt in our faces. My brother went to work in the fields, and I would have liked to do the same, but my ankle was paining me, so I was forced to stay home and suffer the lively abuses of my mother, all lazy this and rascal that.

By afternoon, I found Leela rinsing her feet at the pump. She drank a palmful and wiped the glisten from her chin. Her gaze came to rest on the laundry line where the wind was billowing into Jayan's blue mundu, the one she had been holding as he was carried off by the Karnataka police. I waited for her to speak of what she had seen, but she was preoccupied with the mundu, staring so hard her gaze could have burned a hole through it.

Then she sighed, as if giving up. "Manu, help me with that thing."

I limped to the laundry line and took up one edge of the mundu while she stepped back, holding the other. The fabric was damp and pliant, not yet stiffened by sun.

We tugged opposite corners as she had taught me years ago when I was her household deputy. "There were three men," she said finally. "Drunks. Dancing on the body."

"Of the Gravedigger?"

"As if you don't know. Right corner."

I nearly dropped my end. "You think we—" She thinned her lips. "But we weren't in the forest last night, not anywhere near it! Ask anyone, Sabu, Shaji . . ."

"A clever couple. You could've been tumbling in the belly of a whale for all they'd remember."

"Believe me—"

She tugged so hard, the fabric jerked from my grip. "Just give it here." She took up the mundu and brushed off the small stones, then folded it by half and half again. "What kind of place is this, where men dance on the back of a god?"

I withheld the answer, knowing she was in no mood to hear it.

A place where the gods dance on ours.

Later that day, Leela told my mother she was going to church, an alibi my mother accepted with sympathy due to her own history as a young and unhappy wife.

Leela took her time pinning the pleats of her polycotton sari just so. Usually she kept her plastic mirror canted at the ceiling, reluctant to be reminded of her sun-speckled face. Dabbing kajal under her eyes, she felt something shift in her belly. She had felt no such motions since the Gravedigger's attack. Now her hand went to her middle, searching and hoping until a belch escaped her—gas and nothing more.

She had not expected to get pregnant so quickly. During her years as Podimattom Leela, she had done abortion three times, and that was after a slew of home remedies—long peppers, papayas, mutton-marrow soup, running her belly into the back of a chair. No woman's womb could survive such abuses unharmed, which was what she told Jayan after he proposed marriage. He laughed and said his soldiers could survive any terrain.

Back then, she was what they called "a family girl"; she only made hotel visits as arranged through her agent, an aunt in Kottayam. Jayan was the first she had brought to her home, the first to compliment the cushion covers she had sewn, the first to meet her gaze when she spoke. How strange to think she had yielded her heart simply because he had looked her in the eye, yet this smallest of gestures made her feel important and even a bit powerful. Where was that power now? She was shackled between land and sky, always looking down at the soil or up for rain.

And then she saw the dying elephant, which was not the Gravedigger, which was smaller than the tusker she had faced. Touched its grainy skin and inhaled the rot. Stood mere feet from the flaccid trunk, the enormous arm of a god outstretched. Not her god but a god all the same.

Fifty-six gods. As far as they knew.

Leela told herself she had made the appointment with Madame in order to seek out a job for Jayan—that was all. In her mind she dressed him in the greens of the greenbacks, pictured him proudly patrolling the forests and taking people on tours, the sort of job where cameras were the only things capable of shooting.

Leela stood face-to-face with an old fossil of a greenback. He looked up from his desk and fixed her with one wide hawkish eye, the other a milky slit.

She drew an important breath. "I have an appointment."

The fossil showed her to Madame's doorway and retreated to his post. Madame had a phone clamped against one ear; in the other she was digging a bobby pin, routing out the wax with a militant look. Noting Leela, she tossed the bobby pin aside and gestured to the seat opposite.

Maps of the region sprawled across the wall behind Madame, bristling with red and yellow and green pushpins. Leela twisted the corner of her handkerchief around her finger till the tip went cold.

"Hah, sir, thank you, sir." Tired, impatient, Madame dropped the phone into its cradle. "An elephant was slaughtered in Sitamala. I'm sure you smelled the carcass before I did. Shot in the chest, shoulder, leg, they made a bloody sieve of that creature—eh eh! Hallo?"

Leela had closed her eyes through a sticky wave of nausea. She nodded as Madame hollered for water and tea.

"Isn't this your second trimester? The nausea should have passed by now."

"It comes and goes," Leela managed. Secretly she was glad for the sickness. It served as reminder that the baby was alive.

The fossil provided them with two paper cups of hot water, a tea bag in each like a dead fish, bleeding brown. Madame took up the tea bag and dipped it thrice. "So. Your husband."

Her husband, her husband, that ever-present subject. Couldn't they start with any other topic—childhood, children, her nausea even? Leela had spent so many days alone with her worries, praying that her baby would survive untouched, dreaming of giving birth to a stone. Some chitchat would have offered fleeting relief.

But Madame was not interested in relief. "Your husband has an associate by the name of Alias. Have you heard that name?"

"Never."

"Slippery fellow. Remarkable aim. He once shot an elephant here"—Madame pointed to the space between her own eyebrows—"and the force was so great the animal fell back on its haunches. Usually the animal falls forward, but this one died sitting up."

As she spoke, Madame opened a drawer and removed the few photographs that lay on top. "Somehow Alias and his associates climbed up and did their work, and when they were done, they left this memento."

Leela lowered her face to the photograph Madame had laid on the desk. It took a moment for the shapes to resolve, for her heart to gather speed.

Slowly she made out the twin gray hills that crowned the head, the flaccid ears on either side, but where there should have been a face was a cavity yawning wide, a maw of cut cords and rutted surfaces, a mulch of crimson and bone. Madame traced two pale ridges that met in a V shape. "Those are the bottom jaws. The back teeth were worn down. He must have been eighty years old. And another time, we found an elephant with only the tusks cut out. That fellow was still breathing when we found him."

Leela pushed the picture away. "My husband is a farmer, not a butcher. Not anymore. He fell in with bad types. He made some mistakes, he has paid." There was a bad weight growing dense in her chest. "Why are you showing me this? You just happened to have it in your top drawer, this picture?"

"Open your eyes." Madame's face was pleasant, her voice of

steel. "Your husband was involved in an ivory route that went from here to Dubai, the details of which I am still trying to learn. He killed fifty-six elephants single-handedly—"

"Who gave you that number? The two-faced idiot who turned him in?"

"—but you see, his last kill is the one that fascinates me. He was perched in a tree when he shot an adolescent male of roughly eight years. A bullet to the back of the head, a clean kill, but not clean enough. Because the mother is there. The mother goes to her dead son. The mother touches her trunk to his. They do that, the mothers, to check for breath. But there is no breath. Your husband waits for her to leave, but she won't. She simply stands there very still from day to night to dawn. All the while your husband waits in the tree. And when it's clear she will never leave, Jayan shoots her too, cuts out his five-kilo tusks, both their tails, and leaves. But here is what I will always wonder—why did she stay? Surely she knew your husband was in the tree. She gave him ample target of herself for one full day. So what was going through her mind?"

Unsure of the question, unsure of everything, Leela shook her head.

Madame leaned forward. "Maybe she was thinking, *I know what you are. And I will not look away.*"

A fly settled on the photo of the headless elephant, scurrying this way and that as if trying to find a way into the carnage.

"Who can say?" Madame sat back with a shrug. "But returning to the point, yes, I agree your husband's associate is a two-faced idiot. Too much an idiot to craft a story like that. And then there were the tusks in your shed. Five kilos' worth.

Not much, but what do you expect from an eight-year-old elephant?"

Leela drowned her gaze in the tea. "Past is past," she whispered. "Why do you scratch at it?"

"So you won't let it happen again. Think of your baby." Leela shut her eyes, but Madame's voice pushed into the dark, into her very heart. "Will he have to bear witness to his father's deeds? Think what it will be like for your child, how it will be to meet his father behind all that chicken wire."

"I think of nothing else!"

"Then?"

"I don't know what you expect me to do. He makes his plans without me."

"I am not asking you to make up a story. Just tell me when you do know something—names, buyers, locations . . ."

Leela's gaze wandered to the maps on the wall. All those red and green and yellow points, a sordid constellation. Each pushpin seemed a crime her husband had committed, a sin she had yet to discover.

Leela addressed the pushpins in a murmur so low Madame had to lean in to catch it. "If I help, you will not touch an inch of him. No beating. No sentence. Just—threaten him. Scare him enough to stop. Arrest him if you must, but only for a night."

"I don't want any more years from your husband's life. These poachers dwell at the bottom of the ladder; they get scraps. Throwing one in jail is of no more consequence than plucking a mushroom—" Madame broke off. "Forgive me, I spoke without thinking."

But Leela was spent of rage. She swirled her paper cup and watched the fish swim round, as yet unaware of how rare it was to exact an apology from Madame. Madame never apologized, for she never made a mistake. Sometimes she regretted a decision, but once decided, she acted, and quick.

As the day wore on, the dead elephant gave off a stronger reek as if a wound had opened in the very air, foul and festering.

I glutted on coffee till my stomach grew upset. Nonetheless, I was determined to stay awake for our meeting with Alias. We would leave for the hunt by five the next morning.

With Leela gone, I busied myself by milking the cow. The rhythm of milk drumming tin might have calmed me at first, but White Girl kept slapping my face with her tail as if I were a vexing fly.

In the late afternoon I wandered over the land that two weeks prior had been harvested. The dirt was brittle and pocked, and soon we would have to seed again. From here I could see all five of my mother's acres; she would will half to each son. And so would Jayan and I divy our plots for the generation to come, on and on, all of us living elbow to elbow, head to toe. I felt my future dragging me deep underground. I thought of my brother and my uncle and the greenbacks and the farmers. I thought of the elephants and the forest creatures, all their vengeful yellow eyes. Let them battle over this dirt, I thought. I was destined for elsewhere, sure as calves become cows.

But how clever can he be, the boy who fails to complete the rest of that refrain? Not all calves will be cows. Some will be supper.

That evening I could hear Leela shrilling at my brother before I had even reached the sit-out, where my mother was planted in my father's wooden chair. Elbows on armrests, her hands hung helpless. She raised her sad old gaze to mine and asked, "Where have you been?"

"The fields. Where else?"

"I don't know. I don't know anything about you anymore."

I pretended not to catch that last part. "What are they fighting about now?"

"Ah," she said, a grunt of surrender. "He says he's leaving. She says she will leave him first. Rice going cold."

I made to step inside, but she took hold of my forearm. "You won't leave, will you, String?"

I had not heard that name since I was a child, when my father picked me up and declared me equal in weight to a string. "Now why would I leave you, Ma? Where would I go?"

"Not me. Jayan. Promise to watch him once I'm gone."

I stepped back. "Did you ask him the same? To watch over me?"

"My boy, you do not need watching like he does. He was always a rascal, always smashing things, scared of nothing. I thought prison would put him right, but there is no right for him now." She winced at the sound of Leela shouting. "The evenings were always bad for me, the evenings never gave me peace."

I was stilled by her words. I turned my gaze upon a gray raft of cloud, hoping she would not see the pity in my eyes. She had no patience for pity.

"Say it, child. Promise me."

I promised to watch over my brother. But my mother's face remained a clench of worry, her hands moving over each other like separate creatures seeking warmth.

"Am I stupid?" Leela shouted. "You think I don't know where you go?"

I found my brother in his room, pulling on a shirt as he looked coolly at Leela or somewhere past Leela, as if she weren't worth looking at.

"Going where?" I asked.

She answered for him. "To meet with his fellow outlaws. To plot another poaching."

"Is it only the elephant you care about?" Jayan said. "You should join the Forest Department."

She hesitated. "I care about my child. What kind of father will he know? A law-breaker? A liar?"

"What lies—"

"I know you killed fifty-six elephants. *Fifty-six,*" she reiterated to me. "Shot by his own hand. Did you know?"

I gave no reply. In truth I had not known the exact figure but had always known better than to seek it out.

Jayan turned his back on us and yanked open a drawer. "Who told you that? One of your fat-mouth church friends?"

"And that last one—a mother and child. Just for five kilos? What kind of person does these things?"

Jayan slammed a drawer hard enough to crack the almari. "The kind who won't waste a good set of tusks. That money kept you happy."

"Oh yes, so happy! And where are these piles of gold, where have you stashed them away? In your little shed? Up the cow's rump?"

"Don't talk about what you do not know."

"I know that you are a dog to these people you work for, who- ever they are. Less than a dog."

I tried to step in. "This is not like that, Leela, this is not for those people—"

"And *you*"—she pierced me with a look—"are a fool to follow.

You think he is doing this for us? For this family? No. He wants to erase the past. Show everyone what a hero he is."

I watched Jayan's fist open and close just as my father's used to do when at the very edge of violence. But then by degrees, the fire subsided, and he retreated deep inside of himself where her words could not reach.

"Come, Manu," he said. "Alias is waiting."

Leela turned to Jayan. "Alias, who is Alias?"

"Manu, let's go."

"Wait." She took a step toward me with a look that said, *You do not have to go, you do not have to do everything he says.* We stood at an awkward distance—not close, not far—through which Jayan strode.

I met her eye. A sorry sigh escaped me.

"Go then," she called, her voice at my back. "Follow your brother all the way to Mysore. See how you like wearing their bracelets."

As we walked, her words rolled around my head. She'd had the face of a careworn child as she spoke my name, and what did I look to her but a traitor? Yet what did she expect? Two brothers side by side naturally fell into step. And how could I, considering the oath I had pledged my sad mother and all the years of our brotherhood, betray my own blood?

All at once Jayan plunged into a one-way discussion. "Had I shot her in the hind parts, she would have tossed dirt on her wounds and charged me. Or she might have run off." A puzzling moment passed before I understood him to be discussing the mother elephant. "Still she would have come back while we were taking the tusks. They always come back."

"What's done is done," I said or some such nonsense answer. But I could tell by his silence that it would never be done, that it would remain forever undone now that Leela knew about it.

The moon was a dead man's eye, rolled back and white. At this hour only men traveled the road, off to meet friends or court trouble. Before Raghu died, I had been no different, light of foot, easy of mind. Bloodlusting elephants had been nowhere in my line of sight.

An express bus came thundering through the dark, high beams ablaze, and though I have stood aside for many such buses, this one charging and bellowing down the road and bearing a sign in the windshield—PARUMALA THIRUMENI PRAY FOR US—chased my heart to a gallop that did not ease until the headlights washed me in whiteness and left me stiff in its wake.

"Manu."

I realized that Jayan was staring at me. He stood some paces ahead, confused. "What the hell are you standing there for?"

"Is the Gravedigger fast as that?" I asked.

"As what?"

"The bus."

Jayan searched my face for meaning. "Maybe. How would I know?"

"I thought you knew everything."

He expelled a sigh as if rueful already for the mess he would put us in. (Ah, if he had known the half!) "You have us confused." He aimed a finger at my chest. "You were the genius. On your way to great things, sure as calves become cows."

The phrase made me smile.

"On your way out of here. Just as he wanted it." It was rare to hear Jayan raise our father from the ashes without an insult attached. "You were his best bet. Only one that would have made good."

I looked away from my brother, glowing in the light of his words. Eventually, as always, we fell into step.

"Remember what he used to say of me? *That Jayan has fewer uses than a pile of shit.*"

"*At least shit can make a thing grow.*"

Jayan chuckled, the two of us oddly warmed by our father's abuses. We drifted into our private thoughts against a rasping riot of night frogs.

"I remember the time you taught me to shoot," I said.

"Did I?"

"In the forest. You set a plastic bottle on a log. You had me fix the back part . . ."

"The stock."

"The stock against my shoulder. You told me to inhale, hold my breath, then pull the trigger. Inhale, hold, pull. I forgot all about fixing the stock. Next second I was on my back and staring up at the trees and you were all *You hit it you hit it!*"

This was one of the happiest moments in all my life, not the moment I realized what I had hit but the second my brother spoke my name. He called me with surprise and pride, called as if to claim me as his.

Jayan snorted. "From what I recall, you had the aim of a blind man."

"I'm telling you, I hit it!"

"I doubt that very much."

"I remember," I said. "I remember it all."

The Elephant

The Gravedigger would never grow comfortable with the lorry. It jolted him over roads that led to festivals and functions and weddings and rallies, while cars and motorcycles swerved about in a red streak of horn. In the lorry, the ground was always grumbling through his soles, as if a storm were nearing.

Sometimes, when he passed through a village on foot, people came to the door with sweets and fruit. These he did not mind, but the crowds, the churning crowds, they swallowed him into their scrum, shoved treats in his face. *Tap, tap, tap* went the Gravedigger's trunk, blessing every bald spot and pomaded dome that approached. Parents nudged their children forward, fearful little things thin as saplings, who came with a feral scent.

Shoals of people pressed in with their awe, their need. The Gravedigger would have borne them better with Parthasarathi by his side, but the elder elephant had disappeared three days before, carted off in a lorry. At every new place, the Gravedigger searched the air for a trace of Parthasarathi, who was nowhere to be smelled or seen.

Heavy the heart and the load, now shouldered alone. The whereabouts of Parthasarathi became the Gravedigger's constant preoccupation, plunging him to anguish during musth.

. . .

Musth was the dark time. Every few months, the Gravedigger was thunderstruck, his body vivid with rage, panting with the urge to run and crush all, down to the last man or sapling. The Gravedigger was fifteen years old, the age at which, in the forests, he would have parted from his clan and taken up with the bulls, who would have taught him how to charge and when to retreat, how to draw a cow from her clan (or read her rejection), and how to cope with musth.

At Elephant Sabu's place, when the Gravedigger was stricken by musth, the pappans kept him shackled between trees. These were tighter chains than the changala that usually hugged his leg; tethered forefoot to hind foot, he could not take a single step. Food appeared in a trough or was tossed to him from a distance by the pappans, who stayed beyond the Gravedigger's line of sight.

On the road, the Gravedigger was ambushed by musth more often than usual. Once, it happened at a wedding. One minute he was carrying a groom through a raucous parade, the next minute he was ripping out a stand of lemon trees, the drummers and dancers scattering like ants, while the groom clutched at the sides of his howdah and squealed.

With front leg and back leg chained between trees, the Gravedigger watched the sun creep across the sky. The trees leaked shadows. He sniffed the rubber of passing tires, the dusty musk of the bird that sat on his spine, snapping up gnats. In the old days,

Old Man would squat on the ground beneath the Gravedigger, his back turned as the elephant twisted leaves into his mouth. Over time, the Gravedigger had learned the shape of Old Man's spine, each stone descending from the last. Every so often, Old Man would hum.

But Old Man no longer turned his back on the Gravedigger. His eyes were wary; he had dropped weight, but a bird on the Gravedigger's back.

With no one to soothe him, the Gravedigger resorted to memory. His mind roamed over the faces and smells he had known as a calf, the flick of a cousin's tail, the sour-milk smell of his sister's breath, a pile of elephant ribs still echoing a faint fleshy scent. For hours he could stand quietly, falling into the past like a leaf drifting to forest floor. Such thoughts detached him from the two trees, drew him inward, drew him home.

§

Two days it took for the Gravedigger to recover from musth, ten minutes to load him into the open truck bed, thundering toward another destination. As evening fell, the smell of his fellow elephants flowed over him from a hundred yards away. He was almost home.

Relieved, he thought of the days to come, the order restored. How he would sleep to the sounds of Parthasarathi's snoring. How he and Parthasarathi would lie beneath the sun as Old Man hosed their sides and legs and bellies, how the pappans would rasp at his skin with a coconut hull, how he would fall into a bottomless nap.

As the lorry rumbled up to his stall, the Gravedigger caught a strange smell leaking from Parthasarathi's stall, where Parthasarathi was not. The pappans leaped out of the cab, stretched. The Gravedigger reached his trunk in the direction of Parthasarathi's stall and recoiled from the foreign odor. A stranger's reek.

The Gravedigger went still beneath a mud slide of realizations. They had taken Parthasarathi away. They had put some other elephant in his place. Parthasarathi was no more.

Down came his trunk upon the lorry's cab. He struck with all his eight tons, deaf to the shouts of the pappans and the rumbles of the other elephants, his screams filling his lungs like water until he had no breath left.

§

They locked the Gravedigger in the lorry for hours, without food. When he was hollowed of energy, they maneuvered him into his stall, Elephant Sabu watching, Old Man leading the way and making gentle sounds.

At some point, impatient, Romeo yanked the chain.

· · ·

The Gravedigger swatted him to the ground. For the elephant, the gesture was little more than a tap; for Romeo, a blow that dropped him like a sandbag. All the pappans stood dumb with dread. The Gravedigger felt a dim flare of distress until Old Man began his lowing again, as if no harm had been done, no punishment looming.

Elephant Sabu mouthed something at Romeo, baring his teeth in threat.

Romeo slunk away, wretched and low to the ground.

§

Unable to sleep, Old Man rose from his cot and went to check on the Gravedigger.

The elephant stood in still silhouette within the four sides of his stall. Old Man kept his distance, unable to say whether the Gravedigger was dozing. Like a nursery rhyme came his father's advice: *An elephant asleep on its feet is an elephant ill at ease.*

He could have smacked Romeo for rattling the Gravedigger so, but what was the point in railing against the toothless buffoon? Elephant Sabu was to blame for the Gravedigger's state. It was Elephant Sabu who had assigned them so many events, stringing one against the next as smoothly as blooms on a garland. He was intent on making back what he'd paid for the Gravedigger, and what he had lost on his beloved Parthasarathi.

. . .

Old Parthasarathi had been riding in the back of a lorry, whose usual driver was home with the flu. In his stead, the driver sent his reckless, rum-soaked sons. The boys sped over a pothole that caused the elephant to slam its head into the cab. After some time, a taxi pulled even with the lorry, the driver yelling out the window, "Pull over, pull over! Something is wrong with the elephant! It is stumbling about!"

Soon as they braked, Parthasarathi fell to his knees, fell asleep.

Putting another elephant in Parthasarathi's stall had been Elephant Sabu's idea, a possible antidote to the Gravedigger's loneliness. Elephant Sabu, too, was saddened by the loss of his favorite elephant, whose photo appeared each time he flipped open his mobile. He canceled Parthasarathi's remaining engagements, returned all deposits. He brought suit against the rum brothers and braced himself for the investigations of animal cruelty brought by the Forest Department.

In purchasing the Gravedigger, Elephant Sabu had anticipated a gilded future, but now each loss seemed a stone in his pocket. His wife urged him to assign the Gravedigger more work. What's the point, she said, of keeping such a handsome fellow at home?

So Elephant Sabu hired out the handsome fellow to temples and churches and wedding processions, even to political rallies, both Congress and Marxist, wherever the organizers would pay a fee. Some of these hucksters shirked on the amount of panna and water they were meant to provide, and there were times when even the pappans went without proper meals. Mani-Mathai made no complaint though his belly gurgled in protest. Romeo regularly threatened to quit.

Anytime Old Man tried to reason with Elephant Sabu, he got a long speech about the costs of being in the Elephant Business— the water, the medicines, the veterinarian's bill alone! Thirty bottles of glucose for Parthasarathi's intestinal obstruction plus four bottles of Hermin infusion . . . not even trying to make a profit . . . simply trying to survive . . .

Meanwhile, the elephant had taken to nodding more than usual, to the tune of some dark, swirling rhythm.

Some of the other pappans took precautions, sneaking opium into their elephants' feed to dull the animals during musth. Old Man would not go so far, not yet, though the Gravedigger's silence reminded him of those early, delicate days in the anakoodu, when the calf flickered between this life and the next. Back then, the calf had latched onto Old Man, and over time, they became two halves of a single conversation. Now the elephant seemed locked inside a separate room.

The memory of Appachen's advice descended on him from time to time, to seek another job, any job. But Old Man had refused; this was the tradition to which he'd been born, a known road that had been cleared for him by previous generations. He had meant to maintain the way, even if no one else did.

. . .

Fool's talk, his father had said. No one wants to be a pappan any-more, not even the pappans. A toilet wiper makes more than us. And a toilet can't kill you.

§

The sky above him wild with stars, and still the Gravedigger could not sleep. He felt a smoldering under his skin, an ache in his tusks, until the breeze brought him the scent of Old Man. That invisible presence, however brief, was a steady palm to the Gravedigger's side.

In time, Old Man's smell receded, his footsteps rasping away.

Moments later, another smell spilled through the darkness. The Gravedigger caught the chemical smog, the liquored stink that filled the mouth like bad fruit.

Romeo emerged from the shadows. He entered the Gravedigger's stall and went about some mysterious business. The Gravedig-ger felt himself being clamped forefoot to hind foot. Something was wrong—the Gravedigger was chained this way only during musth, and in the presence of Old Man. Where was Old Man?

Finished with the chains, Romeo stood before the Gravedigger. His dark shape swayed. The Gravedigger could not see Romeo clearly, nor the pitchfork in the pappan's grip, yet he sensed the world tightening around him, a pressure building inside his head.

. . .

The pappan stabbed the Gravedigger's leg. Pain blazed up his flank, hot and stunning.

The same pain shocked him where the skin was most tender, behind the ear and under his tail, then his side, and his belly. There was no room between one pain and the next, no time to let the hurt breathe, only pain and pain again while the pappan barked nonsense, the aroma of liquor and sourness pouring off his skin. The Gravedigger shrank from the pappan, growing smaller and smaller until he was but a calf again, trying to hide from the hands that were yanking him from his mother's side. Forever on it went, that blur of barking and stabbing until, at last, the Gravedigger smelled hope blooming up from the darkness.

§

Old Man was a magnificent snorer, able to sleep through any storm. Mani-Mathai, meanwhile, sought refuge beneath his own pillow. Even a slender, plipping leak in the roof could keep the boy wide-eyed for hours, so the elephant's shrieks brought him running. And what he saw and heard stopped him dead in the darkness.

Is that what you want? *Is it?*

With every question, his uncle speared the elephant's side.

. . .

His mind gone blank, Mani-Mathai let two stabs pass in this manner before he rushed forth and kicked his uncle in the back of the knees. Romeo drunkenly flung his arms and elbows, but an easy blow to the ribs reduced him to a fetal position, hands over his face.

Mani-Mathai stood up and was flooded by the old fear of fathers and whippings.

Romeo rose, stooped, his hand on his side, his voice shrill with disbelief. You broke my rib, you stupid ape!

I'm telling Sabu Sir. In the morning, I'll tell everything.

Go on! his uncle sneered. He'll tell you that's how we do things! We break the animals! You think we charm them with caramels? You think Old Man did it any different?

He wouldn't.

You would defend him to the death. But who will defend you when the beast comes charging?

The boy looked to the elephant. It was either heaving or nodding, he could not tell which.

Romeo took a deep, pained breath before he spoke. Let me tell you something. You want the elephant's friendship, but you cannot be both friend and master. An elephant is not like a cow or a horse, you cannot tame it fully. Some part of it will always be wild. That is the part you cannot trust, the part you have to break again and again.

Mani-Mathai stared at the pitchfork lying on the ground. Secretly, he had always wanted his uncle to speak to him thus, as an equal, not a nuisance. But these were not words he wanted to hear, even if they carried a glint of truth; they stung.

This is our job, said Romeo. This is what we do. Now who is in charge—you or him?

The boy picked up the pitchfork, weighed it in his hands. Go, he said.

Go what? Are you even listening to me?

Go! said Mani-Mathai, and took a swing at his uncle. He missed by inches, but it was enough to send Romeo fleeing into the night.

The Filmmaker

The rot reached for miles, penetrating windows, breaching walls. It wormed into the nose and burrowed deep, no match for mouth breathing, as we drove straight to the molten core.

Teddy rode shotgun, camera fixed on Ravi, who slouched in the opposite corner. Bobin sat in the middle, knees all pinned and prim as if contact with my boom mic would be unseemly. I asked an obvious question just to get them talking—"So where are we going?"—from which Bobin abstained by leaning back.

Ravi wore the slack, haggard expression of an inmate. He was in no mood for questioning, let alone a question he'd answered not two minutes before while the camera was unfortunately off. "We are going to the postmortem of a dead elephant in Sitamala. The goal is to ascertain the cause of death and, if it was a poaching, to recover the bullet and file a case with the police."

"What if you don't find the bullet?"

"Police will not even look twice at the case. Everyone is depending on me to find it: DFO. ACF. Chief Wildlife Warden." I waited, letting Ravi's mind leap ahead to other tangents. "The worst thing is when the bullet is in the head. The inside of the head is all tunnels and cavities, like a honeycomb. It can bounce this way and that, go anywhere . . ."

"Do you think it's the same elephant who killed the boy in Sitamala?"

"No. I told you already." He dragged a hand over his face.

"The Gravedigger is a tusker over three meters high at the shoulder. This one is smaller—we can tell from the circumference of the footprint. There is no connection."

"But the Gravedigger definitely killed the boy in Sitamala."

"It seems so, but . . ." He shook his head. "It's strange for the Gravedigger to come back here, after so many years."

"The bamboo might have something to do with it. Like you said."

"Could be that. Could be he knows you want to film him and it's making him crazy."

Bobin cracked a rare smile. Teddy held on Ravi's face for a moment, about to lower the camera until I asked, "Have you ever seen the Gravedigger?"

We were rounding a bend where a hank of long grass, growing almost horizontally from the hillside, reached through Ravi's open window. Absently, he ran his fingers through the strands. "Long time ago. Back then he was called Sooryamangalam Sreeganeshan. He was the most famous temple elephant. They put his picture on calendars, postcards; there was even talk of putting him in a movie.

"My whole family went to see him at a festival. All these nine elephants they squeezed into a temple that could fit only three. There was so little room, the elephants were leaning against one another, and because Sooryamangalam Sreeganeshan was the tallest, he was in the middle. All through the blessings and the prayers, he was nodding and nodding, at nothing. I asked my mother why he was doing that. She said he was happy, he was hearing a song in his head. Can you imagine? Only a bhranthan would be nodding like that."

"Bhranthan?"

Lost in thought, Ravi squinted at the window, as if all nine elephants were nodding in the distance.

"Madman," Bobin clarified.

The dead elephant loomed huge and unreal, like a parade float partly deflated and collapsed on folded, rubbery limbs. Its chin lay on the dirt, its trunk outstretched, the corners of its mouth drawn up in a perverse little smile.

Ravi and Bobin began by zipping up their raincoats. They slipped on rubber aprons, wriggled fingers into gloves. Another assistant, taking extra precaution, clamped on a motorcycle helmet.

They found and photographed the burnt, black spot of the bullet hole on the elephant's side, behind the left shoulder. But the bullet was far deeper, a baby dragonfly buried somewhere in that bulk of flesh.

Teddy closed in as Ravi wormed a stick into the burn hole, trying to assess the vector of the bullet. Bobin brandished a metal detector, sweeping the air around the wound until it began to bleat frantically. Across that spot, Ravi traced a *T*.

With an X-Acto knife, Ravi sliced away a square of dermis, thick as a house mat, and peeled it back. Beneath was a shiny layer of fat and muscle, marbled with pink, and in the center, the burn hole like a black star that had bored its way through the flesh, spiraling, widening a contrail as it went. Teddy and I stepped closer. The stench of pus filled my mouth.

They took a saw to the animal's side, the sound like a zipper going up and down. With pliers, they pinched and sheared the muscle beneath in great, gleaming swaths, blood pooling up. They cut around the huge wet balloons of organs, searched the medusal knots of the small intestine, cauliflowers of calcified fat.

Hours passed, and still no bullet.

By four o'clock, the heat had baked the stench to new heights. Teddy and I stepped away from the carcass, taking a break to switch out tapes, when Ms. Hakim came striding down a narrow berm, a handkerchief held to her mouth, followed by a forest officer with glinting badges and a mustache thin as the swipe of a knife. She surveyed the scene—carcass, Ravi, Bobin, guards—until her colorless gaze came to rest on us. I waved. She ignored me.

Putting a hold on the postmortem, Ms. Hakim summoned Ravi aside. She conferred with him quietly, and he nodded in response until something she said made him stop nodding. He scanned her face, then the ground, seemingly at a loss for words. They hung there, suspended, no longer a scene but a freeze-frame of something vital, something we would miss entirely if Teddy didn't hurry with the tape.

As soon as we rose to join them, the conference was over. Ms. Hakim and Ravi parted ways, him to the carcass, her to us.

"Teddy. Emma." She stuck a peremptory smile on her face. "You must be tired. Let me take you back to the center."

I glanced at Teddy, both of us reluctant. "Oh—well, we'd prefer to stay until they've wrapped things up."

"They are wrapping things up, I told them."

"Then we'll just get a ride with the team," I said.

"No, they must drop off the tissue samples at the lab and then they must meet with me."

"We could film that," Teddy suggested. "The meeting would be an opportunity—"

"No," Ms. Hakim said, adding a kindly grimace, as though it pained her to cut him off. "No filming in the meeting."

"So that's it then?" I said. "No bullet? We're giving up?"

Ms. Hakim nodded, oddly at peace with the outcome.

I looked at Ravi, perched atop a stepladder, arms sleeved to the elbow in slush. He paused, called out: "Go ahead. I will see you at the center."

On camera, we got Ms. Hakim to tell us that the bullet had not been recovered, that the carcass would be guarded overnight and burned tomorrow. As soon as Teddy turned off the camera, she motioned us to follow. "Now come, please come. The smell is too much."

Less than a quarter mile from the elephant, Teddy insisted we stop the jeep so he could set up the tripod for one final shot— the raw, violet surge of mountains, the hill of dead elephant in the foreground. The rest of the way, he tried to bait Ms. Hakim with questions, which she met with a face flat as a wall. I kept quiet, simmering with the sense that we were missing a crucial piece of the story and that Ms. Hakim would be the last person to disclose it.

The next morning at the center, Ravi was nowhere to be found. I left him four text messages that began cool and curious, then spiraled into urgency. I skipped breakfast and logged tapes, just to keep myself busy.

Teddy ambled in and flung himself across my bed, poorly suppressing a belch. "Bobin's mom made cutlets for us."

I tapped the space bar, freezing on a frame of Ravi midsentence, lips pursed. Normally I would have leaped at the possibility of cutlet: crisp breaded shell, warm minced meat. But today my stomach was knotted up, all nerves. "I can't eat right now."

"Would you relax?"

"I am relaxed."

"Your leg is having a seizure."

I stilled my knee. "What do you think he's hiding?"

"Something good, I hope. What're you so wound up about?"

"It would be nice to know he's being honest with us."

"Maybe he's not an honest guy. Maybe that's what makes him an interesting character."

But to me he was more than a character. And I felt I deserved the truth; his honesty was a measure of his respect for me, proof that I wasn't some forgettable chick he'd bagged during a lull at work.

"Emma. You okay?"

I blinked at the screen. "This shot's a little under. Little dark."

Teddy rolled onto his side, squinting. "Yeah. Damn. All that white wall in the background. I should've cropped some of that out."

"This bit is gold." I tapped the space bar, and Ravi came to life.

. . . *so the animal that primitive man most feared was the tusker with the broken tooth. These were the angriest, most irritated creatures, most prone to very violent episodes. So why do you think primitive man chose to worship Ganesh, an elephant with a broken tooth? Because fear and worship are two sides of one coin.*

§

Around noon: the rusty squeal of the gates. Teddy sprang from the bed, where he'd been daydreaming behind *Documentary in the Digital Age,* not a single page turned in the last half hour. We grabbed our equipment, hustled out the door.

"Exam room," said Teddy. Before I could suggest we meet Ravi at the jeep, Teddy was off.

The exam room was empty when we set up in the corner, farthest from the entrance. "He always stops here first," Teddy whispered.

"We should tell him we're filming."

"It'll be good to catch him in a private moment."

"But it's kind of an ambush—"

Teddy shushed me like a schoolmarm and told me to keep the boom low.

We waited, and I thought of Helen Levitt, snapping her way around New York, armed with the winkelsucher that allowed her to peer over other people's shoulders. Usually the small, frail shoulders of children.

Ravi didn't see us immediately. He dropped his bag on the counter. He fell into a chair against the wall, elbows on knees, hands limp. His stare seemed to go on for miles, minutes, unblinking. Out of the corner of my eye, I caught Teddy adjusting the zoom, zeroing in, a gesture that induced in me a small spasm of loyalty. I cleared my throat.

Ravi's eyes snapped up and caught us. There's one Levitt photo I can recall in which a child seems to resist Levitt's attention. A frowning girl of maybe fourteen, rings under her eyes, a stitch of contempt between her brows. She meets Levitt's gaze, distrusts and detests it. This was precisely the gaze that Ravi was giving us. "What the hell are you doing there?"

"We wanted to film you coming in," I said, avoiding Teddy's glare. "We thought it might be more authentic this way. Without you knowing we're here."

Ravi went to the sink. "Turn it off. I don't want that on me right now."

Ting! and the camera closed its ogling eye.

Teddy and I stood there, bereft of purpose, a pair of sheepish wallflowers. Ignoring us, Ravi unzipped the duffel bag and removed a burrito roll of blades, which he spread across the counter beside the sink. Dull silver on scarlet felt. I looked closer; some of the blades were laced with blood.

"Wait," I said, though Ravi kept moving, turning on the faucet, adjusting the water to a soft patter on steel. "Did you just get back from the postmortem?"

"Yes. We found the bullet this morning."

"The postmortem you were wrapping up *yesterday*?"

He ran a bar of soap through his hands and nodded.

"But Samina said you were disposing of the carcass this morning."

I stared at the back of his head, the thick swirl of hair. "I decided to keep looking. I told you, the bullet is very important."

"Why didn't you wake me up?" I could hear my voice going shrill, too furious to care how the question might've sounded to Teddy. "Why didn't you take us with you?"

"You filmed all day yesterday," Ravi said. "I thought you'd be too tired."

"Thanks for your concern."

"What is the problem? It's a good thing I found it."

"What about the meeting with Samina? Why couldn't we come along?"

Teddy stepped in, his voice smooth and pleasant. "How about we shoot you cleaning the blades, Ravi? That okay?"

Ravi consented with a shrug. He ran each blade under the water, pinching it clean with a rag. Teddy shot the red dregs swirling into the drain. Eventually Teddy got him to report that he'd found the bullet, got him to repeat that thing about the head as honeycomb. The entire time, Ravi didn't so much as glance at me, merely slid the X-Acto knife, neatly, into its niche.

The Poacher

Our final task, before tomorrow's hunt, was to meet Alias at a tea shop. Many a man slouched over the long wooden tables, a mess of crumbs and glass cups, some full of chai and some lit with candles whose light played over the ruffled tin of the ceiling. Flies spun circles around a single bulb. Below it sat a big-bellied pan, its sides blackened and whipped by flame.

The air was close with the smell of deep-frying dough, but for once my brother had no appetite. We sat at the vacant end of a long table and spoke in low voices. I could not help but stare at our cohort's puckered stumps, a samosa clutched in the claw of his three surviving fingers. His whiskers glistened grease as he nodded at me. "Is this the third?"

"My brother," said Jayan.

"We need a fourth."

"No. Only us three. Manu can do all the carrying."

Alias gave me an up-and-down look, the same my mother would give to a traveling trinket salesman. "If you say so."

He detailed the point where we would enter Kavanar Park, his fingers tracing our path along the seams in the wooden table. He was in cahoots with a ranger who would allow us passage at the edge of Old Raman's farm (unbeknownst to poor Raman), just east of the dead banyan that had been cleaved by lightning. From there, Alias could track the elephant easily and was miffed when I asked, "How, exactly?"

"The Gravedigger walks with a limp," he said. "His hind leg strays outside the others." Alias reenacted the footprints on the table, crossing one hand over the other. "If the earth is damp enough, it's easy as reading his signature."

"And if it's a dry day?" I asked.

"We keep looking. I've been on trips that take a week."

I frowned at the prospect, but my brother was nodding.

"This is the job," Jayan said. "We will not leave until it's done."

And what if, I wanted to know, this ranger cousin was not as loyal as Alias presumed? Was he a first cousin or three times removed?

"Jayan," Alias said, pinning me with a stare, "have you no other brothers? Even a sister would do."

Jayan hissed for quiet. The samosa man was regarding us from under the hairy eaves of his eyebrows. He scooped out a sizzling clutch of samosas on a slotted spoon the size of an oar and dropped them in the colander.

Alias asked if my brother had a gun. Jayan grunted. As for Alias, he would bring his famous rosewood.

"What about me?" I asked.

"You carry the pack," Alias said. "Bedding, blades."

"No blades," said Jayan. "I told you."

"No blades my buttocks!" Alias leaned in with a scowl he had likely perfected from birth. "Those tusks must be forty kilos at least. You want the Forest Department to add to their collection?"

"I don't care what they do." Jayan looked at the table, intent on avoiding my eyes. "It's not for me anymore."

"It will take thirty minutes max. Thirty thousand rupees. Tell me you couldn't use half that."

Jayan sulked at the cook fire. Alias waved him off with his half hand.

"Is that all?" I demanded. I had hoped for more of a training on tracking or baiting, not out of cowardice but preparedness, as I was in no rush to lose my own digits or anything else for that matter. "Is there nothing more to know?"

"All you need know if something goes wrong," said Alias, leaning forward, "is to run."

Something furry flicked over my feet. I jumped up, startling the glasses just as a stray cat leaped out from under the table, back arched and yowling her indignation. Someone shooed her into the night.

Every bloodshot eye was now cocked and aimed at me.

Alias showed his first sooty smile of the evening. "Getting an early start?" he said, and cackled so proudly at his joke it was clear he had been in the forest too long.

After Alias left, Jayan and I went to a toddy shop where the crowd had the cumulative scent of an armpit. People clapped their hands on my brother's shoulders, crowed his name with great affection. I could see that he was someone here; he was theirs. I was merely his brother, but that title bestowed some specialness on me, and so I basked in their smelly camaraderie.

All night I drank from a mildewy glass. The local brew seared my stomach and made me weightless and careless. I remember the jolly cacophony of singing, saucers of belly-burning lemon achar. I remember waking on the spike of some bony man's shoulder, feeling much heavier than when I began the evening. "We thought you were dead," said the bony man, passionately licking sauce off his finger. "Try the pickle, Wee Shivaram, it will bring you back to life."

I asked after Jayan. The man pointed me to a pair of crooked trees, where my brother was relieving himself. With some difficulty, I wobbled outside and waited—he seemed to be watering the whole forest—and while waiting, I gazed on the clear navy sky, which carried so many stars at once I thought I might finally see one fall.

"They never fall," said Jayan, "when you will them to."

True and yet. It was enough to stand beside my brother, adrift in a single current of silence.

"Shall we go home?" I said at last.

"In a little while."

"We told Leela we would come home soon."

Jayan groaned. "You wouldn't remove a splinter from your own foot without asking her permission." He took a few steps toward the toddy shop and stopped in the middle of the road when he realized I had not moved. "Come on."

"Get out of the road."

"Not until you come."

"But Leela—"

"Your nursemaid? She will be fine."

Normally that sneer in his voice would have cut me to half size. But between my achy head and my shifty stomach, I had no interest in holding us together, the duty that always and entirely fell to me.

"I am going home," I said.

"Don't be touchy, we were having fun!"

I began walking away; he rushed me and slung his leaden arm around my shoulder. I threw it off.

His face cooled to indifference. "Go to her then. You are the one she wants. Always saying how smart you are, how lucky the girl who will get you."

I told him to stop his babbling even as I was desperate to hear the rest.

He peered down the road as if he could see his future looming large in the dark. "My wife has no need of me."

"That is for her to decide. Not you."

"You heard her. What am I good for anymore?"

"You work on the farm same as me."

"She could find another day worker for that. And a day worker would come with none of the fuss she spends on me."

"Enough, we have to get up early tomorrow."

"In jail"—Jayan shook his woolly troubled head—"I thought I would come out changed. But then I came out and I saw that the world had changed. And I had stayed the same."

All at once I was a child again, fearful, searching the wasteland of my father's face, the gullies of his eyes.

"Stop this song and dance," I said. "Let's go."

"You go."

Unsteady on his feet, he shambled toward the distant embrace of drunken voices. He felt far from me, as unknowable as a figure in a fable.

I staggered home.

Obviously—and yet it must be said—I had no plan of trysting with my brother's wife. Nothing like that. I only knew I wanted to prove something to Leela, and this intention pulled me stumbling through the moonlit roads. The liquor dragged my feet.

At some point a spiteful tree lifted a root and felled me smack on my face, and I felt the whole forest itself was colluding to impede me.

Impeded I was not. I washed my feet at the pump before entering the house. Leela emerged from her room, greeting me in a voice gentle as dewfall—"You've come?"—and I thought surely she had forgiven me. "Where is Jayan?"

"Coming," I said, my lips feeling unnaturally thick. "He is coming. Later."

"You left him?"

"Isn't that what you wanted?"

She folded her arms. "Now you care what I want?"

I began to protest, but she shushed me and glanced toward my mother's room. "I need something to drink. Come sit with me."

I thought she meant to have a cup of warm milk, not my mother's gooseberry wine. She poured two glasses and placed the bottle on the kitchen table between us. My mother was very proud of her home brews and refused to listen when we begged her to experiment with a milder fruit. One whiff and this one would pucker the whole throat.

Leela seemed to have no qualms. She downed a glass at once and closed her eyes as the wine stole through her like an old song. In this shut-eyed state, chin in her hand, she began to tap a pattern on the surface of the table, and I looked on her as I had never looked before, with an open kind of ardor.

Her eyes met mine; I held her gaze. Who knew gooseberry wine could be the very elixir of audacity? If she wanted to ask me why I was staring so, if she was keen to know the true nature of my deep-down feeling, so be it: I was ready to confess.

"He is planning something, isn't he?"

Of course I was crestfallen by her question. And surprised too by the ease in her tone, given her earlier hoopla. "He will stop after this one."

"He will stop when teeth grow out my nose." She burped impressively and patted her chest. "When are you planning to go?"

"Why do you want to know?"

"Why do you think? When Madame comes round again, how will I lie to her without knowing the truth?" Leela sat back, much offended by my hesitation. "Do you think I will blabber to the next fishmonger that comes along?"

"We do not get many fishmongers."

"You know my meaning."

"You may blabber to Ma, which would be worse."

"I did not blabber about your girlfriend."

"Girlfriend? Which . . ."

Her mouth went stern. "Never mind which. Do you trust me or not?"

"Yes. No." At that hour she could have convinced me to eat mulch, such were my powers of reasoning. "We leave Wednesday. Tomorrow. At dawn."

She poured me more. "You and who else?"

"Fellow named Alias."

She blinked at the name, three times fast.

"You know him?"

She shook her head.

Leela was keen to know every particular, from where we would enter to what we would eat, which I suspected were merely symptoms of a wife's busybody curiosity. "You know the dead banyan on the edge of Old Raman's farm, the one split by lightning? From there we will enter." Time to time she nodded dimly as if only half attached to my words.

When the bottle was empty, she turned it around in her hands. She murmured something about tiny ships being raised within bottles like this. I was not listening in full. My eyes were on her belly, gently insisting against the front of her nightdress.

"Does it kick?" I asked.

The question took her by surprise. "Just once," she said softly. "Never since."

"Give it time."

She contemplated me with those heart-gripping eyes. For once they were free of reproach, only hopeful, as if my words held the power of premonition.

I should have stopped there. I should not have scooted forward in my seat, should not have asked, "Can I?"

Her brow furrowed. Shame arrived, belated yet crushing. I willed her to raise the bottle and crack me unconscious.

But then she clasped her hands below her belly as if cradling a gift.

Slight as it was, her nod was an invitation.

I sat on the edge of my chair and placed both palms on the firmness of her middle. She held very straight and still and I could feel the boy, I could feel him stirring and turning as if to greet me. Maybe such fetal motions would be deemed medically impossible by higher minds, but what is the language of science where the mysteries of life are concerned? I was captivated by the finger-length boy. I was captivated by his mother too: the smell, the velvet feel of her. So many years of want plus whiskey and wine will make a beast of any man, though I have no excuse for what I did then. There is some I do not remember, but I remember her hair, her smell, something sodden and wild around her neck, and a sourness to her cheek, and though I knew her face, the salty angle of her throat lay bare and new to me. This close, she was nothing like I had imagined and yet perfect. She was everything, everything.

She whispered a few words I did not catch. I withdrew my face mere inches from hers.

"Make him stay," she said.

I leaned back to look clearly upon her features. Her eyes, so dreamy a moment ago, had turned dark and desperate. I withdrew, but she clutched my arm. "Talk him out of it. You are the only one who can."

I recoiled from her brittle fingers, sought support from the edge of the table. Her face was a miserable plea. She would do anything. Anything.

I stumbled out into the night. I heaved my innards onto dirt, my stomach in revolt, expelling everything but the memory of her eyes when I backed away, how they turned tired and resigned in the way of old widows.

Soon afterward I surrendered to sleep. I suspect Leela stayed awake for some time. I did not see her remove Samina Madame's business card, which she had kept in the tin beneath Jayan's prison letters. I did not hear her pick up the phone with trembling hands, the dial spinning like the cylinder of a gun.

I am sure that Leela wanted only to scare my brother. She did not want her baby to inherit her own sufferings, and there was not a thing between heaven and hell she would not do for its sake. Her actions would cause many to call her a snake and a traitor, but they did not hear what awoke me later in the night, her weeping and weeping without knowing this was only the prologue to her sorrows.

The Elephant

On the boy's birthday, Old Man bought him a Choco-bar. Mani-Mathai lapped at it so slowly and carefully the ice cream began to melt in sticky ribbons down his wrist. He saved the stick and set it on the ledge above his cot, which had so recently belonged to his uncle.

Aside from this, the day resumed its routine. Feeding, resting, mucking, bathing. With Romeo gone, replaced by one of Parthasarathi's pappans, the very air seemed to loosen. Why he had left, no one could say, but Old Man noticed that the departure gave way to a fresh affection between Mani-Mathai and the elephant, whose trunk arched in question whenever the boy came near. Once, Old Man watched the boy reach up and place his hand on the side of the elephant's face, as if in reassurance. From this gesture, Old Man saw there was something Mani-Mathai was not saying, perhaps to do with his uncle's sudden exit.

§

That afternoon, the wind blew so strong, Mani-Mathai felt he could sit on it and sail away. This remark drew a smile from Old Man, who told him to sail off to the kitchen and get some coconut husks for the bath.

. . .

Mani-Mathai was trotting across the yard when Romeo's voice, sudden as gunshot, stopped him.

Boy!

Mani-Mathai turned slowly, uncertain. His uncle was ambling down the drive, grinning with his too-perfect teeth. A blue plastic bag swung from his hand.

It's your birthday, isn't it? Look—I remembered.

Romeo dangled the bag like bait. Mani-Mathai asked what was in it.

His uncle fished out a brightly colored package with the word BULLET emblazoned in red. You like firecrackers, don't you? These will make your heart jump out your mouth—

Old Man won't allow crackers. He says the elephants get enough noise at work; they should have some peace at home.

Since when do you obey his every order?

Since he gave me your job.

Romeo lost his smile and suddenly the boy understood why his uncle had returned. How sorry Romeo looked, how deflated without the drink to puff him up. He had lacquered his hair with a pomade in order to make himself more presentable, in the unlikely hope of regaining his old position. He smelled like a fruit-flavored candy.

Mani-Mathai had no plan to help his uncle, though he had not disclosed to Old Man the incident with the pitchfork, fearful that doing so would invoke some twisted form of revenge and maybe the meddling of his father. And in small part, he was afraid that Romeo was right, that Old Man might endorse the use of pitchforks.

An awkward silence passed, filled only by the sound of Romeo scratching his fruity scalp. Well, he said. I don't give a wet fart for Old Man's orders. Boys should be boys, I say.

He held out the blue plastic bag.

I have work to do, said Mani-Mathai.

Just take the blasted thing. It doesn't bother the elephants, I'll show you—

But Mani-Mathai was already walking away.

§

By evening, the sky had turned a jewel blue, lighter at the edges, rich at heart. The Gravedigger was being led back toward the stalls, freshly bathed and drowsy. The bath had doused him in the sort of peace he had not known in weeks, lying on his side with the water rivering over his belly, Old Man humming, husks scratching, and the song joined with the scratch in a rhythm so soothing the Gravedigger fell asleep.

Now he was eager to eat from the mounded panna that awaited him. But a wrong whiff was gusting from the direction of the stalls, something foul and familiar.

Darkness seeped into the periphery of his vision. He was desperate to flee that smell. He wrung his head lightly but kept walking, urged on by Old Man.

As they neared the stall, the Gravedigger scented Romeo. The pappan who had stabbed him, who might force him into the stall and stab him again. Who was squatting over something on the ground.

A sizzling smell: sulfur, match.

The boy took a few running steps forward, shouting at Romeo.

Romeo leaped back from the thing on the ground, baring his teeth, plugging his ears. A plastic bag drifted and whispered in the wind.

A fuse, hissing like a plague of cicadas . . .

And then, the bullets.

. . .

In the end, what broke the Gravedigger's mind was not merely the *stab stab stab* of the firecrackers, nor even the sight of Romeo. It was the pomade coming off the pappan's hair, the sticky pineapple rot that slid through the air and up his trunk, shocking his head with a memory from a day long ago, the day his mother roared and sank, the day her thud ran electric through the earth, the day the gunman walked away with her tail—a sticky pineapple rot wafting off his hair.

All the days between then and now collapsed.

Shadows piled like ash at the edge of the Gravedigger's vision, closing around his target.

§

Run! Old Man yelled, chasing after the Gravedigger, who had broken free of the changala and was now charging at Romeo.

The other pappans scattered, as Old Man would have done were it not for the fact that he had lost sight of Mani-Mathai. Through the maelstrom, Old Man shouted for the boy.

It happened in moments, unfolding beyond his control, so that all Old Man could ask of his fate was: *So soon? So soon? So soon? So soon?*

§

The Gravedigger snatched up Romeo in his trunk and slammed him twice against the side of the stall, until his head went loose as a fruit about to drop. The Gravedigger felt someone yanking on his chain, igniting his abscess. He stumbled back— a muffled grunt beneath him—and felt the easy crush of flesh underfoot.

By now, the bullets had stopped, but still the singed smell.

A muttering came from down below. It was the boy, who had run up to Old Man, who was not Old Man, who was a limp, dead thing. The boy fell to his knees by the dead man's head, placed a hand on the dead man's cheek. He recoiled as if scalded.

His eyes traveled up to the Gravedigger. A moment of stillness passed between them. What was broken could not be mended, neither for Old Man nor for the elephant.

The boy's eyes went small with anguish. He rocked and bowed and held Old Man's head as if he meant to take it away. But it was for the Gravedigger to take the body away. It was for the Gravedigger to restore the silence of all things.

Lifting his foot over the boy, this is what he did.

§

Once there was a clan who came across a pile of bones, picked clean by birds. The bones had belonged to a young cow they had known, and the adults took turns sniffing and cradling her remains. Still a calf then, the Gravedigger had stood between his mother's legs and watched as she dipped her trunk into the hollows and sockets of the skull. A deep-sea murmur in his ears. This was how he learned to grieve the dead.

The memory came back to him as he wrapped his trunk around the pappan's ankle and pulled him next to the corpse of the boy, trailing a dark sweep of red. Old Man was last. The Gravedigger touched his breathless mouth and locked that smell in some chamber of his brain. Then he curled Old Man into his trunk and laid him across the others. He covered the bodies in panna leaves before limping toward the mountains.

§

In the forest, wild elephants wanted nothing to do with the Gravedigger, not with the death stench of man tattooed into his skin. He would pad quietly to the watering hole, where a clan was taking rest, but as soon as they caught the tidal stink of his coming, they shrieked and clamored away. Even the forests had changed over the years of his absence, blighted by dying bamboo, patched with green and gold farm.

No sight was stranger than the treeless swaths through which he and his clan used to cross, taking shady refuge beneath the ribs of the trees. Little remained of the rosewood and aanjili, only stumps like rivets in the earth.

On hot days, the abscess on his ankle throbbed like a second heart, inviting a musth that left him shrieking and tearing at the trees. The bouts were fewer and farther between, but each time the noises invaded his thoughts and drowned him in fury.

Those were not his final killings.

The Gravedigger thought of Old Man more often than he thought of his own mother; the recollections passed over him slowly, throwing shadows. He remembered Old Man's musk, fresh upon the air, the stepping-stones of his spine. How he hummed at times. How he appeared in the anakoodu that very first morning, his sun-dark body in the white square of light. The Gravedigger's mind ran back and forth between now and then, a depthless stream of memory.

Only when he entered the lake did his mind go still. Underwater, a hush entered his body. His limbs cycled freely, almost as though he had never worn the chain around his ankle, as if he had never known that weight.

The Filmmaker

On Friday, the villagers stormed the Forest Department. They came by the hundreds, they came with their kin, blocking the highway, shaking their fists and shouting at a pitch that pummeled the speakers of our twelve-inch television.

Teddy and I were nesting in a mangy love seat with our tiffins of rice and dal. For the last half hour, Bobin had been filling out monthly reports, sickle-bent over Ravi's desk. When the news story began, his gaze darted up. He hadn't blinked since. The anchorwoman spoke in a breathless stream from which I caught one word—*Sitamala*. Bobin squinted, leaned forward, shushing me every time I asked for a translation. His pen hung in the air as if he were frozen whole, aside from his thumb, which kept clicking the tip.

"A poacher was shot by forest officers," Bobin explained, still squinting. "The same poacher who killed the elephant from the postmortem. There was some kind of scuffle . . ." Bobin paused to listen, his whole face scrunching up. "The officers say they shot him in self-defense."

"So why are the villagers protesting?" I asked.

"The villagers say that poacher was not responsible for the Sitamala elephant. They say he was unarmed when he died." Bobin snorted, shook his head. "Even though he was carrying the same type of bullet we found on the Sitamala elephant."

"So what's their theory?" Teddy asked.

"They say we are conspiring with the Forest Department. They say we *planted* the bullet on the man's body. What kind of nonsense . . ."

Planted: the word sent a jolt through my gut. I turned back to the TV, where the anchorwoman sped through the rest of her report. Several times, she mentioned a "Mr. Shivaram" beneath a shot of a sweaty, disheveled man leading the others, the cords in his throat pulled taut.

"Who is that?" I asked.

Bobin glanced at the screen. "Must be the dead man's brother."

The Poacher

Wednesday, well ahead of sunrise, we commenced our journey as a party of three, sidling through an opening in the tree line. We wore green half pants and black undershirts so as to camouflage our bodies and elephant shit on our arms so as to camouflage our smells. Jayan and Alias moved nimbly but I was burdened by a pack crammed with too many items: a tarpaulin, four clean shirts (to blend into the public posthunt), cartridges, bullets, binoculars, torches, matches, bidis, gram, rice, sambar masala, meat masala, black pepper, chili pepper, and salt.

I had accused Jayan of overpacking: Why so many masalas? Should we bring cinnamon and saffron too?

"Have you ever had plain wild meat?" he shot back. "Goes down like wood pulp."

Already I was dreading our meals and was reminded of that dread each time a monkey shrieked. These were the milky hours of morning when the howlers and prowlers were scuttling in the trees, cicadas hissing like a lit fuse. All my life I had known such sounds, yet now they rang eerie and foreign in my ears.

How strange then to see my brother so sure of himself. He moved with the silky certainty of a panther stalking prey, the way his feet never faltered, the way he plucked his shirt off a snagging branch so as not to leave evidence of his presence. His face was sharp and intent, hardened by heartache. To his mind there was only one way the hunt would end.

Alias led the way, carrying his trusted rosewood and a pack much lighter than my own. His eyes swooped in on every dropping and pug mark. He knew the paths of the patrollers and the crackle of their walkie-talkies, the location of the antipoaching camps. He caught every breakage of branch, whose pure green heart meant the snap was fresh and recent. The fellow did not know dental hygiene but truly he knew his business.

We skulked through rattling thickets and phantoms of mist, a slice of raw pink at the sky's beginning. Tall towers of tiger bamboo leaned over us, some brown and dying and scribbled over by vines. The damp earth muffled our steps. Had it been a dry day, any crackling leaf could have betrayed us.

At times we heard a shudder among the bushes, and we froze, barrels leveled at the noise before moving on. It was morning and the herds were on their way down the mountain and into the valleys to drink and bathe at the lake. By afternoon they would trail back up the slopes to the golden open scrublands, a higher altitude where only a scatter of bush and evergreen still grew. There we would stalk the Gravedigger.

Several hours passed, and my back begged relief of its burden. The silence suited me even less as it set my mind wandering toward my performance from the prior night. Sometimes the memory crept up—sticking my nose in her neck like some lecherous mutt—and made me spasm with self-hatred.

So I was grateful for the distraction of a morning snack. We shared a tube of biscuits and a flask of water, which sent me in search of a private spot, my business being of a substantial nature. My brother called after me unkindly, "Don't get lost."

I wove around a few trees, plucking a handful of leaves for hygienic purposes. In my desire for privacy, I ventured a bit far.

I found a discreet little clearing and lingered over it a moment. I had never voided myself upon forest floor, and for the tenth time that day I asked of myself, *How in hell did Jayan do these things?*

I dropped my half pant and squatted. Instantly my bowels went on strike, demanding better conditions. I imagined my brother aflame with impatience, tromping through the forest in search of me. I doubled my efforts. At last, in sore defeat, I yanked up my half pant, preparing myself for Jayan's ridicule, though what came first, what froze me tip to toe, was the throaty rumble rising behind me.

I turned by degrees.

The Gravedigger stood a few yards away, its body obscured by bamboo, its tusks reaching white through the vines, its head looming and vast as a cliff.

Sweat stung my eyes yet I would not blink. I stared at one of the tusks, the tip that had long ago gored a man's galloping heart.

Running seemed pointless and beyond my power. My legs were limp, my hands empty, aside from a fistful of sanitary leaves. I prayed to the tusker as had every numbstruck luckless clod to face a rogue thusly unarmed. *Finish me quick.*

Aside from an ear twitch, the tusker did not move. Its legs were granite columns, supporting such a spectacular bulk. It regarded me with its honey-hued eyes as if to take my measure, my potential for harm. As I stood there, I felt an odd calm settle over me. Fathoms deep, those eyes, small inside the cliff sides, close to the color of my own. Remote and ancient. Eyes that had seen the wild and not-wild, eyes that knew things.

The whole forest seemed to hold its breath. All at once the Gravedigger came to a conclusion that caused it to turn and saunter off, thrashing aside a tree as if it were of no more consequence than a weed. Thus the Gravedigger departed, quiet as it came, a cool gray moon. It had let me live.

I ran.

Branches slashed at my arms, vines whipped me in the face. Surely I was making a show of myself, gasping and huffing through the trees. When Alias reached out of the green and snatched my shoulder, I nearly yelped. He and my brother looked most incensed, Alias going so far as to bare his black gums. "What were you doing out there—giving birth?"

Jayan said he had gone looking for me. "Where were you?" he demanded.

I took a long trembling breath and imagined the tusker standing in judgment, weighing my fragile self, and something inside me shifted. Jayan's gaze roved over me like a torch. For reasons I could not discern at the moment, I skirted the truth and mumbled instead: "Constipated. I am constipated."

I turned away and shouldered the pack. Alias stuck his snout in my face. "You can shit a brick for all I care. We are on serious business here—"

Jayan put up a hand. "Enough. He understands."

Alias looked between my brother and me, baffled by Jayan's calm. I suspect my brother had intervened not in order to defend me from name-calling but because he had caught a secret wafting off me and knew pressure would best be applied in private.

Alias tossed Jayan's hand away and said we would have to double our pace up the mountain in order to meet the Gravedigger on the slopes as planned. He trudged first, me second, Jayan last, my brother's eyes boring into my back. I clenched my hand to keep it from shaking.

The Filmmaker

As soon as the news report ended, Teddy and I headed back to his room. He was utterly confused. He begged me to debrief him on what the hell Bobin had just told us and, more important, what he'd left out.

"So two days ago," I said, "an elephant was killed in Sitamala."

Teddy nodded impatiently. "And yesterday morning, Ravi started the postmortem."

"Right, and sometime during the postmortem, this poacher, Mr. Shivaram—he was killed by a forest officer. The officers took a bullet off his body—"

"Out of his *body?*"

"Just listen. The guy was carrying bullets. One of those officers must've taken a few and delivered them to Ravi, and he, sort of, maybe . . ."

"Planted a bullet? On the dead elephant?"

I nodded.

"Jesus."

"Allegedly. We don't know what Ravi did unless we discuss it with him."

"Oh, we'll definitely discuss it." Teddy paced the room in militant strides, his hands stuffed in his armpits. "We'll film him on his rounds tomorrow morning, and then we'll end by asking him about the dead poacher."

"What, like, out of the blue?"

"I also want to raise the question of corruption. Something

like *How do you feel about working so closely with a Forest Department that's been accused of a massive cover-up?* Which could lead to a discussion of the Shankar Timber case . . ."

I listened in silence, staring at the splayed Moleskine on his desk. Teddy was talking with his hands. I took a breath, braced for impact. "I don't know."

Teddy halted. "Don't know what?"

"The whole gotcha approach didn't work so well last time."

"I thought you were all about spontaneity. This could be a pivotal scene."

"We'll just piss him off."

"Better than getting a canned answer. We pissed off Samina Hakim; you didn't care about that."

"We don't need her the way we need him. Seriously, I think it'll go better if I talk to Ravi first."

"Let me guess." Teddy eyed me steadily. "Alone?"

"He gets defensive sometimes, when we're both there." Teddy snorted; I persisted. "I won't ask for specifics. The shoot will still be spontaneous. But I think it's only fair that we let him know we want to go down this road."

"And if he says no?"

I shrugged. "Then no. It's not worth hurting him."

"How would our little film hurt him?"

I hesitated; Teddy read what I couldn't say.

"Shelly was different," he added quietly. "She completely misinterpreted . . . she thought she was in love with me." He paused. "Or maybe it's not that different."

My stomach tensed.

"Emma, is there something you're not telling me?"

That had always been my line, during interviews. At first I

felt the pinned, panicky sensation I must have inflicted on others, but then the panic subsided, displaced by annoyance. What got me was the trickle of condescension, the indirectness of the approach, the sting of Ravi's comment: *He treats you like a child.*

"Nothing you don't already know."

Teddy squinted as if he'd misheard me, until the truth seemed to crystallize, slowly, before his eyes.

"You and him," he said.

I nodded.

When it became clear that I wouldn't elaborate or apologize, Teddy stared hard at the ground.

"It's over," I said. "Obviously. We're leaving in a few days."

"He could tell someone. A blogger could pick it up. We'd never make a film again."

"Now you're being melodramatic."

"How are you supposed to be objective now? How the hell am I supposed to trust you?"

I hesitated, unaccustomed to the scorn in his voice. "Ravi won't say anything."

Teddy shook his head.

"I know him, Teddy."

"You slept with him. There's a big fucking difference."

A glacial silence passed as we stood there, suspended between strangers and friends.

I said I was going, but he didn't lift his head.

In my room, I brewed black tea to stay awake; it went down in a bitter flame. I could've waited till morning, but my head felt so clogged with suspicion and dread I had no room for patience. I needed Ravi to tell me that what we'd heard was simply untrue, and until then I wouldn't sleep.

Later, I found Bobin by the jeep, overseeing two keepers as they lifted a large wire cage from the back. Inside was a small macaque, munching on a banana.

"Ravi?" I asked. Bobin pointed me to the exam room.

The hanging bulb cast a sinister glow in the center of the operating table. I didn't notice Ravi at first, sitting in the shadows, the same pose we'd caught him in the day before. Hands hanging empty, face vacant.

"Hey," I said, causing him to bolt to his feet. "It's just me. No camera."

He weighed me a moment, then went to the table and unlatched the plastic toolbox, setting vials aside like a weary bartender.

"I saw the news." I tried to sound casual. "I heard about the protests." No answer, no sign of recognition. "We'd like to interview you about it." More vials, more bottles. "And we'd like to interview those farmers about what happened, maybe Officer Vasu too."

"Why them?"

"Because it's important to show how the local community perceives you. And the center." I felt the villagers' accusations vying for space in the room. "Those are some serious allegations."

"There are many sides to the local community and most of them are supportive of us. What you are trying to sniff out is a handful of rioters."

"What happened?"

"Confidential."

"Did Samina make you do it?"

"Make me?" His laugh came out flat and fake. "What do you think she is—a gangster?"

"Did she give you the bullet in her office? During your confidential meeting?" As I spoke, he stepped away, turning his back on me. "Is that why she hustled us out of there, why the postmortem just *had* to continue the next morning?"

"You people." He locked onto me with slitted eyes. "Always hunting for a story so others can watch and feel outrage. What about my outrage? What about the outrage of another dead elephant, one I might have pulled from a ditch or a cave and brought here and bandaged and bottle-fed with my own hands? Plucked like that, easy as a weed?"

"I just want to know what happened."

"You want to cut me open and drag it all out." He clapped the toolbox shut, shelved it under the table. "Isn't that what you do? Isn't that your gift?"

"Tell me what happened to the dead guy. Shivaram."

Even with my butchered pronunciation, the name made Ravi stare into the surface of the table, at the bright smudge of light. The whole room seemed to go still, and I kept silent, sure that one word from me would cause him to snap.

He said the poacher had been killed a few hours after the postmortem began. Officer Vasu had been involved. Some kind of confusion with the poacher, guns fired. "Vasu was frightened. He is one year from retirement. So he went to Samina Madame for help—"

"And she came to you."

"She said to suspend the postmortem. That same night, I came to her office, as she asked. She explained the situation and gave me the bullet."

"Where'd she find the bullet?"

With difficulty, Ravi said that Vasu had gotten it off the body. The man had been carrying a pouch of bullets but, mysteriously, no gun. "She gave me the bullet. She said it was up to me."

"To frame a dead man," I said.

"He was not an innocent. Whatever he was planning to do, Vasu stopped him from it."

"He was unarmed! He hadn't done anything!"

"What would you do? Throw old Vasu in the street, let these human rights people make a meal of him?"

"I wouldn't falsify evidence, sorry to disappoint you. That's just fucked up. That's some LAPD shit."

I'd lost him at LAPD. "You cannot put this in your film."

"Why not? Everything you just said is already in the news."

"So why blow it up even further? For your film? So you can parade around and pretend your art is of help to anything but your own career?"

I'd been calm this long, but now rage sprung up in me, hot and quick. "You never had a problem with my art when it made you look good."

He hovered a moment, uncertain. "Forget about me, then. What about Samina Hakim? We never had a DRO like her before. We work closely with her department. Why go after one of the good guys?"

"Her track record isn't exactly spotless."

"Shankar Timber was one case—"

"Sure, until the next timber company comes along or mining company or mill . . ."

"Oh, spare me the lesson, Emma. No one here is a saint, not even you."

"I'm not trying to be a saint. I'm trying to be objective."

"Are you? Then what about the watch on your wrist? You think it appeared out of nowhere? You think that metal didn't come from a mine like the one you're talking about?"

"What—" I glanced down at the ten-dollar Casio I'd gotten from Walmart and crossed my arms. "What's your point?"

"There has been no one better than Samina. I did twenty postmortems in '97. This year I have done two. You want to go backwards now?"

"Oh, for god's sake, the whole future of the species doesn't hang on me."

"No. Nor me." With his thumb, he rubbed at a scratch on the steel table. "I know I am bailing water from a sinking boat with only my hands. You can either help me bail or make another hole." He looked up at me. The scratch was still there. "Which will it be?"

I turned away, but he stepped closer, so close I could feel his breath on my shoulder. I could sense him willing me to yield, not unlike the night he put his hands on my waist. It had happened two weeks ago, but nearly every hour since, I'd hoped it would happen again.

"Please, Emma."

He took my hand. He rubbed his thumb over the knot at my wrist, and for a few moments, we stood like that, avoiding each other's eyes.

Once, in an interview, Ravi had told me he'd never marry, or, at least, he'd never find a woman willing to accept what he called his first wife—the Rescue Center. At the time, I'd thought he was joking. But I saw now that he was committed to something larger than the center, to a panoramic sense of peace, even if it meant painting over certain patches.

Maybe I yielded because I saw the logic—ugly but necessary— in that peace. Maybe I thought I was doing my small and noble part, protecting the species. That's what I'd like to believe, though it seems equally possible that, at twenty-three, I gave in solely because my hand was in his.

I said I was tired, that I'd speak to Teddy, though I sensed Teddy wouldn't be speaking to me anytime soon. Ravi offered to walk me back to my room, but I shook my head, thinking there would be other nights, that this wouldn't be our last.

The Poacher

As we walked on through the forest, I could not rid myself of a certainty—the Gravedigger had let me live, but next time it would not. Every step up the hillside was a step in the wrong direction. My terror mounted; my heart jumped at each twitch and swish of leaf. Time to time I whirled about, surprised yet relieved to see the suspicious face of my brother.

"What is it?" he hissed at one point. "What did you see?"

How I wanted to tell him and would have, had we a moment alone. Even then he would have thought me soft and sentimental as a drunk. He would have guessed the Gravedigger, being weak-eyed, had not seen me, that the smeared scat on my arms had kept him from sniffing me out. Or that I had merely faced a dim-witted elephant, not the Gravedigger itself.

But I had looked into the creature's eyes. Dim it was not.

"Manu," Jayan whispered. "Tell me."

Over his shoulder Alias cast a wary eye. I ignored my brother, my fearfulness, recalled the oath I had made to my mother. I kept an eye on the trees around me, the secrets behind their leaves. The birds gibbered invisibly.

Once we reached the uplands, Alias and Jayan climbed trees, hoping to catch sight of the animal. I stood at the foot of Jayan's tree, scanning the yellow smears of grassland surrounding us, the tiles of farmland down below, the hostile peak up above. Where was the creature? I felt a muscle jumping in my jaw, my mind aswirl.

"Eh! Wee Shivaram!"

I startled, and looked up.

Jayan was frowning down at me. "Binoculars."

"I cannot."

"Cannot what? I know I packed them."

I took off my pack and set it on the ground. "I cannot kill the elephant."

Jayan glanced at Alias, who was glaring all owlish from his perch, close enough to sense a disturbance, too far to hear details. "No one is asking you to kill it."

"I cannot face it again."

Jayan dug deep into my gaze. "What do you mean *again*?"

Alias thunked out of his tree like an overripe fruit, making his way to us.

"What if it knows," I whispered quickly, "what if it knows we are coming for it? They say an elephant can sense when it's being hunted. Maybe it will hide. Maybe it will wait for nightfall, hunt for *us*."

How to describe Jayan's disgusted expression? As though I were a leper, as if the tip of my nose had dropped off.

"What is the shitter saying now?" Alias asked. He struck a casual pose and lit a bidi.

"He wants to leave," Jayan said.

What I wanted was to take the second chance the tusker had given me. What I wanted was to live, to work, to know the weight of a wife on my lap, to watch my children tumble down mounds of rice if life would so bless me. I had never stood in such intimate company with a wild bull elephant or felt its breath steaming upon my face, had never watched the ground beneath my feet fall away until all that remained was the small patch on which I stood trembling. How could a man survive such a thing unchanged? How could he glimpse that unholy omen, a warning as ancient as the oldest of fables, as obvious as a black-bellied cloud, and ignore it?

"Let him," Alias said. He lifted his bidi into the air so the smoke could tell him the wind's direction. "Although you may meet the Gravedigger on the way home."

"How the hell is he to go home? Should he ask a greenback for directions?"

"You could come," I said. "Part of the way. Or the whole way."

Alias shook his head. "I can shoot the beast, but I cannot butcher the thing alone."

"What butchering . . . ," I said. Jayan sighed with exasperation and looked away.

The truth gored me slow.

"But there are no blades in my pack," I said.

"Check mine," said Alias, flicking his chin at the tree where his smaller pack dangled from a branch. "You'll find a kitchen knife, an ax, a handsaw . . ."

"But you told her," I started and stopped. Still Jayan would not meet my gaze. "Where will you hide it? And if she finds it—"

"Enough questions!" Jayan said. "Why must you always be itching and whining, *what if this, why that*? If you are going, then go!"

I looked away, brimming with hurt and fury. Jayan was the type who did not know the difference between humbling and humiliating another. I was fed up with both.

"Then I am going," I said.

Jayan nodded as if he understood this to be the only way. "Go," he said calmly this time. "Go safely."

He offered the rifle, but I refused it. I pretended to remember the route we had taken and promised to carry stones in my fist, lest the Gravedigger should discover me.

"Don't take chances now," Jayan said.

Spent of advice, he bit his lip—how like a boy he seemed then! We had no words, and so we simply looked as we had not looked in a very long time. Think of the last time you looked on someone you loved, merely looked without speaking, a face more familiar to you than your very own, a face that holds such mysteries.

"Our guest will be here any minute," Alias said.

Abruptly I turned and walked away, fleet of foot without the pack. And yet every step felt heavy.

To hunt is to read a hidden language. Inside the forest, I was hunting for a way out. My plan was to take an eastward path, following the kinks of the stream all the way back to the split banyan where the ranger cousin would allow me safe passage. And yet no matter how hard I strained I could not hear the hum of the stream.

I minded the signals: the heaped hill of scat, the sever of a green-hearted branch. I tried not to think of my brother (thereby thinking of him constantly), and thus distracted I lost my footing and snapped a thick twig underfoot. I had snapped several by then, so I thought nothing of it—a sound one would only hear if listening precisely for this.

By now you know: someone was.

The Filmmaker

I barely saw Ravi in those last few days at the center. The middle ground of friendship was strange and swampy terrain, so we kept to our separate banks. I didn't think we would ever be pen pals. His e-mails had the brevity of a haiku, the bluntness of a road sign.

As for Teddy and me, something had ruptured between us, irreparably. He went quiet in my presence, ate alone. We skated by on silence and small talk. I told myself some time apart would be cure enough, but deep down I sensed that our friendship wouldn't survive these final days. Nor would our film.

The day Teddy and I left for Manaloor was a hectic rush of good-byes. Ravi had insisted on trucking the calves in the evening, which left Teddy and me to fret over the fading light. We filmed the calves trailing the head keeper, Tarun, who backed up the ramp and into the truck bed, dangling bananas. Dev seemed especially agitated, immune to the sedative that Ravi had administered, a shot behind the ear. Only when Tarun lowered his head, allowing Dev's trunk to fondle his neck, did the calf grow calm.

Once the calves were shut into the truck bed, Ravi stepped back, ducking to catch a glimpse as they nosed the slats, desperately flexing their nostrils. Something in the way he bit his lower lip reminded me of the way Juhi stuffed her trunk tip into her mouth. His theory was that she did it to keep ants from running up her nostrils at night. I thought it was her version of thumb sucking, a means of reassurance. "Always looking for a story," Ravi had said, not without affection.

Later, I would think of a dozen other ways to say goodbye, jokes about Dev's soccer stardom or genuine words of gratitude, but when Ravi approached I simply took the hand he offered me—a dry, priestly grip, as meaningless as the handshake he'd given to Teddy.

"Emma Lewis," he said. He'd never spoken my name before, first and last, tender and taunting, and the sound of it closed the space between us. I don't remember what I said; all I know for certain is the way he spoke my name, and suddenly it seemed possible that I could return to this very spot, years from now, and all would remain unchanged.

Of course, the illusion lasted only as long as the handshake. As we rolled away, Teddy cranked down the window on the passenger side and adjusted the side-view mirror. It was the perfect parting shot, with Ravi shrinking from view, lost to the swarming green.

In Manaloor, another rescued calf joined the three, a burly number named Bhim. Over the course of two weeks, the calves were taken for daily walks at the edge of the wildlife park, groomed to grow accustomed to the area, taught which berries and leaves to eat. All the calves were fastened with radio collars. Each day, they roamed a bit farther from the rangers, even so far as the watering hole, but always returned.

Teddy let me shoot more than usual during our time in Manaloor, maybe because he knew he wouldn't be using very much of the footage. It was Teddy who would edit the film, Teddy who would score and sound mix the final cut. At first, we tried to work side by side from his apartment, but by then the bitterness between us had grown roots, and rather than fight him every day for reasons far messier than aesthetics, I withdrew myself from the film. I let him have everything. Another six months passed in a pointless blur, the price of surrendering a whole year of my life.

Five years later, I came across our film at the library. I didn't recognize the title—*Kavanar's Creatures*—but the DVD cover caught my attention, a still of an elephant calf with a shock of orange mohawk. I watched it alone, on a library computer, as if containing the film to a ten-inch window could limit the impact.

There was Ravi. There was Officer Soman sparring with Officer Vasu, keepers feeding calves, and Samina Hakim pressing her lips together with muted fury. There was the dead elephant, its skin peeled back like the pages of a book.

There was no mention of the poacher, an omission that relieved and depressed me. I tried to remember his face from the news report, but it was just one of so many images floating past. I snatched at them, tried to align them with my memories.

Teddy had taken very few of my suggestions, but the one that stands out to me still is the final sequence of the film. In it, we're tagging along with a beat officer named Vinod. He's been charged with driving around the park for any sign of the collared calves, who have been vanishing for longer and longer swaths of the day.

One evening, we find the calves on the far edge of the watering hole, where a herd of females is drinking and bathing. It will take the calves another few weeks to detach from their keepers completely. In time, the beat officers will report sightings of Bhim, wandering on his own, while Juhi, Sunny, and Dev are foraging within ten yards of a herd. The officers will find the collars along the elephant routes, ditched like molted skins.

Vinod claims he can see the collared calves through his binoculars, but even through our telephoto lens, zoomed all the way in, the calves are indistinguishable from the rest. They seem twenty-four blots of a single herd that has gathered every evening, for ages, by the lake. And though this feeling has struck me more than once during filming, my heart lifts, open to the world, to the promise of my potential, to the beauty of our making, and I know this is where the film should end. This is it.

The Poacher

Twenty minutes into the forest, I was lost. Each trick my brother had taught me of tracking seemed to bend and blur in my head. What seemed elephant scat one moment seemed bison droppings the next. Did the circular track belong to females and the ovals to males or the other way around? I found a heavy stone—weak defense against an elephant—and upon storing it inside the pocket of my half pant, found something there already.

The bullets.

My stomach fell. I could not go back now and return the pouch to Jayan. Likely he had enough on his person. He had said to me once, *A good hunter needs only one.*

Still. It would give him cause to harangue me upon his return. Of all my possible futures, this was the brightest: Jayan swaggering through the doorway, bloodshot eyes full of triumph and ridicule. And so we would return to our bickering selves.

The longer I wandered, the likelier it seemed I would spend the night in the forest. I fought my own panic. I focused on my surroundings: a parakeet streaking through the air, a red spill of orchid on the side of a sal tree. At its base grew a froth of white mushrooms. I knelt to pluck a handful, a sorry offering for the women waiting at home.

It was then I heard him. A rustling behind me, so brief I would have assigned it to a monkey had I not heard the same rustle earlier that day, as sharp a threat as the squeal of a knife.

I did not risk a breath. Instinct flowed hot and fast as current from my brain to every edge of my self.

I slid my hand into my pocket, closed my fingers around a stone the size of my heart. Shivering leaves. Sunlight. Life moves at such speed, and yet that moment held the whole world still.

I spun about, arm cocked.

What came next is not so clear, for even the brightest mind is terribly slow.

I did not hear the greenback yelling.

I did not feel his bullet pierce my brain, easy as thread through a needle. Only after the bullet burst the back of my head did the tissues, strained to their limit, tear.

With that pure rush of freedom, I left myself.

And then I was running running through the green daze of the forest leaping over grassland in flying strides stopping only to look upon my brother who at the crack of the bullet had dropped out of the tree and screamed my name. Alias held him back—*be sensible,* he said—claiming the greenbacks would never wander so far up the mountain. For a long time my brother squinted into the tree line and my love for him filled the whole of my being.

Yet I could not stay. On I ran and suddenly I knew the way to the stream. I followed it out of the forest and through the farms, over our rice fields where my feet left no tracks and into the house and through the curtain of the room where Leela stood at the window, searching for us.

To meet her eye again. To thread her a needle, to help her fold a sheet. To turn back the days and unmake my mistakes.

I laid my hands on her belly as I should have the night before, with reverence.

I am sorry. I felt the child stir to my touch as did she. *This one, I will never leave. I will watch him always.*

Her hands searched the surface of her belly. The baby nudged her palm.

And now, dear girl, I ask your forgiveness as well. For we speak of boy children before the baby is born as if to bend fate to our favor. Everyone prays for a boy child, but what we needed was you.

I would be there when you were born into a house of mourning; I would be there to watch my brother hold you for the first time, towel wrapped and tight as a loaf in his arms; I would watch everyone carry you around on their hips. You would spend so much time in the air, your mother would fear you might never learn to toddle. But toddle you would, and I would be there to see it. Night and day I would watch you, unable to shield you from the arrows of grief, as when your mother would grow soundless at the thought of me or when your grandmother would stop her own heart as one would still the hands of a clock because she deemed it her time, she being a woman of great authority.

All these things had yet to pass. For now, Leela kept her hands in place, her palm still glowing from that tiny sign. She would name you Manusri—Manu for short—a name that no one could bear speak aloud in your early days, so they called you by other, sweeter names.

§

Now does your mind ever drift back to me? Or am I only the skinny fellow in the portrait that hangs in the sitting room?

That photo does my visage no justice—I appear flat-faced and doomed, when in truth I was annoyed to be late for school. What to say. There is no telling what tales and traces will survive us.

Time to time you pause in passing, your gaze yearning up the wall to my face. Maybe you picture me following your father through the fields or milking the cow or sitting in the palli. There are only these glimpses like a fire that sparks but will not catch.

Someday you may come across the news articles that my brother clipped and collected in his mission to clear my name. What a great hoopla he made. In the reports, I was called Victim. Suspect. Poacher. My death became a cry of protest, something to put on a sign, severed from the whole of my life.

Still I have no hatred for the elephant. Time or man will hunt it down, though few have seen the creature of late. It wandered into one village where the women hurried onto a roof and welcomed it with pots of scalding water. A deaf girl saw the Grave-digger bashing a jackfruit against a tree. She and the elephant met eyes before it dipped its trunk into the flesh, indifferent to her presence.

Among the last to meet the Gravedigger was my brother, but most people think his story too fanciful for truth. This was the Ottayan after all, the beast whose name once appeared in a Western film, who had passed through the rhymes and nightmares of a village entire. Surely Jayan Shivaram had been bewitched by a dream, easy to believe when spending a night in the wild.

.   .   .

All day long, Jayan and Alias searched the forest for the Gravedigger. Jayan struggled under the weight of my pack and his gun, but these burdens were nothing next to the dread in his gut.

As the light began to die, Alias could no longer see the Gravedigger's tracks. My brother refused to quit or go home. I suppose he knew what awaited him there.

So the two spent the night in the forest. They tended a small fire and slept some paces from its dwindling warmth. An old trick: if the greenbacks were to glimpse the fire, they would shoot at the flames, giving Jayan and Alias the chance to escape.

Unable to sleep, Jayan thought about the gunshot. He thought of the fear and pleading in my face when last we parted.

In time, he fell into a restless sleep.

In the middle of the night, he felt the brush of something coarse across his cheek. He blinked to find a pile of branches and leaves drawn across his body. He caught a hint of the swampy breath. He knew.

Before him rose the Gravedigger, sudden and silent, enormous. It was pulling a palm frond over Jayan's chest just as it had done for the still-sleeping Alias, whom the tusker had mistaken for dead.

At last the Gravedigger stopped and hovered over my brother, its tusks dimly aglow. Jayan barely breathed. He could read nothing in the Gravedigger's eyes, aside from the moonlit glint. What did its silence mean? Was it stayed by the smeared scent of dung on Jayan's arms or the sourness of skin and sweat not unlike the scent of my own?

See him there: my brother, buried and breathless at the base of a tree with only a thought in his head. *So Manu was right.*

And with this thought comes another, a realization that chokes him slow. The rest of his life is coming for him with all its grief and bitterness. He closes his eyes and wills the elephant's foot to take him first.

Acknowledgments

My thanks to the Wildlife Trust of India for its invaluable work in the field of conservation, and especially to Vivek Menon, its founder and president, for his immense help with this book. I owe an equal debt of gratitude to Jose Louies, officer in charge of the Enforcement, Assistance, and Law Division. For more information on WTI, visit www.wti.org.in.

I would also like to thank:

The United States–India Educational Foundation and the Fulbright Program, especially Neeraj Goswami.

Abhijit Bhawal, veterinary surgeon with WTI's Mobile Veterinary Service in Upper Assam, whose stories of animal rescue deserve an entire book unto themselves.

Babu O. S., a true encyclopedia of pachydermal knowledge.

Surendra Varma, one of India's leading elephant researchers, who generously organized my own research trip to Wayanad and put me in touch with several warm, intelligent hosts— Mr. Gangadharan Mangalassery, Vinayan P. A., Aparnadevi P. A., Sujin N. S., and Sabitha C.

The Periyar Tiger Reserve, especially Sanjay Kumar Ayyappan, deputy director; Binoy C. Thomas; Manu Sathyan; and Shashi Kumar. By employing former poachers, Periyar has cultivated a small army of expert forest watchers, many of whom gave me their time and knowledge, including Malaichami, P. Deivam, Mahamaya, and C. Pandyan.

Additional thanks for the guidance of the following individuals: R. V. Lakshmi Ammu, Devna Arora, Dr. Jacob V. Cheeran, Carol Buckley, Dilip Deori, Suparna Ganguly, Laban Gogoi, Dinesh K. J. and K. M. Javanayyan Gowda, Bulu Imam, Justin Imam, Divisional Range Officer Shajana Karim, Pratap Bhanu Mehta, Manju Menon, Mahesh Rangarajan, P. V. Subramanian, Subramanyam C. K., and Susheela Varasyar.

These publications were important to the writing of this book:
Elephants on the Edge: What Animals Teach Us About Humanity, by Gay Bradshaw
The Elephant Graveyard, by Tarquin Hall
Deeper Roots of Historical Injustice: Trends and Challenges in the Forests of India, in particular the chapter by Ashish Kothari and Neema Pathak: "Conservation and Rights in India"
Elephant Days and Nights, by Raman Sukumar
"Elephant Poaching in Bandipur Tiger Reserve, Southern India," by Surendra Varma

Thank you to the extraordinary Nicole Aragi, for her generosity and faith and elephant-shaped gifts; to Jordan Pavlin, for lending this book her brilliance. To Duvall Osteen. To Caroline Bleeke, Brittany Morrongiello, Ellen Feldman, Annette Szlachta-McGinn, and the wonderful team at Knopf. To Jenny Assef, Peter Hlinka, and Karen Thompson Walker, kindly readers and friends.

To the Maru family and the James family, to whom I owe a debt beyond words.

To Vivek Maru, who infused every page of this book with his insight and care.

And to Luka, who arrived with perfect timing.